Gathering Frost

Praise for Gathering Frost

"My favorite thing about this book is the action. Jade isn't a sleeping princess. She's the best fighter and so fierce in her "empty" state. I felt like this was an urban fantasy with all the steam of a romance."
- Jessie Potts, *USA Today 'Happy Ever After Blog'*

"Davis writes with confidence and poise, and the story's many twists and turns stave off predictability and allow readers to become immersed in a starkly magical world filled with last hopes."
- *Publisher's Weekly*

"Gathering Frost is just awesome in every way. Beautiful prose, lots of heart-wrenching emotion, action and romance, a great, unstoppable villain, and a smart, tough heroine who will fight for what she wants."
- *Geeks In High School*

"It's well thought out and it unbelievably magnificent. I seriously couldn't put it down. Wait I never actually put it down. I started and finished in one sitting because it's just that good. This one is a MUST READ."
- *Happy Tails and Tales*

Gathering Frost

Once Upon A Curse Book One

Kaitlyn Davis

All Works By Kaitlyn Davis

Once Upon A Curse
Gathering Frost
Withering Rose

Midnight Fire
Ignite
Simmer
Blaze
Scorch

A Dance of Dragons
The Shadow Soul
The Spirit Heir
The Phoenix Born

A Dance of Dragons – The Novellas
The Golden Cage
The Silver Key
The Bronze Knight
The Iron Rider

To my family for their unconditional love,
my friends for their overwhelming support,
and my fans for their incredible enthusiasm.
Thank you from the bottom of my heart.

One

The world ended on a Saturday in spring. Beautiful. Sunny. The sort of afternoon that pulled New Yorkers from their hibernation, urging them to shed their floor-length coats and stiletto boots, to let the sun kiss their pale skin once more.

When the earthquake began, my mother and I were in Central Park. "Pedal!" I remember her shouting. "Pedal!" And I did. My little legs pumped in circles, my heart lifted as I felt her fingers release the bike, and suddenly I was riding on my own. For the first time. The breeze whipped against my grinning cheeks, stinging my eyes.

But then the ground shook. The earth began to tremble. And I had no hope. In a flash, I was on the ground, sandwiched against the concrete as screams rose around me. Darkness stole my vision as my mother's arms encircled me, hugged me closer. Teeth chattering, I tried to be strong. But tears leaked from my eyes, the cries of a baby. Shame burned my chest.

Time passed but my young mind had lost count. Minutes. Hours. I still don't really know. But when the ground stilled, I woke to a new world.

My mother was frozen with shock, so I had to pull against her hold, straining to see. Over her shoulder, south, I saw smoke and ash rising like clouds over my skyline. The trees looked gray, the sky washed out. Faint outlines of buildings were only just visible through the fog, a mix of skyscrapers still standing or leveled to the ground.

I looked at my mother. Her arms had fallen mutely to her side. I'll never forget her green eyes, pulled so taut I swore they were about to snap. Her lips were just slightly open.

"Mommy?"

But she didn't hear. Something behind me had her so transfixed that even her only child, her little girl, could not shake the alarm.

So I turned.

New York was gone.

Like a line driven through the ground, we stood on one side with the past while our future rested a few feet away. A future that was backward in time.

Atop a hill, a giant castle rose from the ground, surrounded by green lawns where apartments used to stand. At its base were stone houses, smoking from fires. Horses. Carriages. Carts. And people. People dressed in dull brown clothes looked at us just as we looked at them—confused and terrified.

And then she appeared.

Her gown sparkled in the sun, brilliant red popping against a dull backdrop, cinching in at the waist and then expanding into a magnificent skirt billowing in the breeze. Silky white gloves encased her hands. Jewels dripped around her thin neck. Pins held her hair so that it curled elegantly down her back, and resting right above her forehead was a golden crown.

My eyes went straight to her.

A princess. I knew she would save us. I had seen it before, so many times, so many princesses saving the day.

I ran to her, crossing the threshold without hesitation as my mother screamed at me to come back. My mom was an adult. And adults didn't believe in these things. I knew she would see my side if I could just get the princess to help us.

She knelt as I approached. A wide inviting smile spread across her face. Her arms caught me.

"What is your name child?" Her voice was warm. It soothed me, relaxed me, filled me with hope.

"Jade."

She brushed my bangs from my forehead, kissed it softly.

"Would you like me to help you? To make all of your fears go away?"

"Yes!" I wanted to run to my mom, to show her she didn't need to be afraid. The princess would help us. But I couldn't. Something stopped me.

A hand pressed against my chest, pricked my skin.

I looked up at the princess, struggling to break free of her hold, when a freeze snatched my heart, so cold that it burned. I tried to speak, but I was frozen. My limbs grew heavy, my lips felt fat, my vision started to spot.

"Don't worry, little Jade. I'm just putting you to sleep for a little while. You'll wake up soon."

I did. In a cell with other frightened girls. But I never felt the same. Icy. That's what some of us started calling it, this feeling like our hearts won't thaw. Even a fire doesn't warm me. I am hard. Frigid. Emotionless. Sometimes I think I must still be caught in a long dream.

But time has only made me tougher.

Now I know the princess by another name, Queen Deirdre, the Ice Queen.

And I wish I could say I was the hero of the story. A resister. A rebel. Someone who lived to bring an end to the queen who stole my childhood—my mother, my life, my very world.

But I'm not.

I'm not the good guy.

I'm the one who puts the good guys in their graves.

Two

The city is silent, full of shadows cast by moonlight. I should be used to it after spending so many hours on the wall, protecting my home, guarding its sleeping citizens. And I am. But sometimes in my dreams, I can still remember the way the skyline used to sparkle outside my window, a blanket of stars close enough to touch.

More than a decade has passed since the city that never sleeps was last awake. More than a decade of darkness.

I hardly remember how easy it used to be, how much we took for granted. Lights were just one flick away. Movies danced on screens before our eyes. Food stayed chilled, the entire world was a few keys away. Honking cars and rattling trains once filled the air, and now they lie still like skeletons, fossils in a broken down museum.

I was only a little girl then. I'm a much different woman now.

"See anything?"

"No," I yell back, rolling my eyes. Of course I don't see anything.

The war has been over for years, long before I joined the guard, but still we keep watch every night, waiting for the rebels to return.

I've walked this perimeter a thousand times, gun at my hip, sword in my belt, crossbow strapped to my shoulders. My fingers itch to swing a blade or pull a trigger, but silence is the only thing that has ever been beyond the wall. Silence and the tap of my impatient feet on stone.

I can count on my hands the number of times I've actually seen a rebel and if they do manage to come this close, there is not much fight left in them. Not enough for any fun anyway. The queen's powers are strong, strong enough to make even the most willful soldier drop his weapon.

I've only heard rumors of the war. I was still with the other children in the dungeons below the castle when the rebels came, still caught by the queen, still waiting for her to determine what to do with us. The sound of smattering bullets is about all I remember. But on the wall, conversations always drift back to the glory days of the war, when the guard had a purpose, when we were victorious.

They say the rebels didn't know how to fight us, how to fight the queen. Their tanks stopped working miles outside the city. Their planes fell from the sky. Long-range missiles simply puttered out.

Magic.

It's the reason the electricity turned off. It's the reason it won't come back on. They say magic has an electric charge of its own, different. One that interferes with the old electricity of Earth. I say who cares. I'm no scientist. And that's not the magic I have to live with, not really.

The magic we deal with every day is what happened next. The rebels marched on the queen's castle a few days after their first strikes wore out. I bet they had no idea what they were walking toward. Machine guns against arrows and swords? I'm sure they thought they had us beat before the fighting even began. But once they stepped into the queen's hands, there was no escape. A few managed to fire their weapons, to take some of the guards out, even a giant or two I've heard. But most just stopped, dropped their weapons, and gave up. Some of those men work beside me on the wall now.

Indifference is the queen's magic. Loyalty to her and indifference to everything else.

More than a decade has passed since I last felt warm. Not like being by a fire, where the flames lick my face and heat presses into my skin. I mean warm from the inside out, like my heart is pumping, like my mind is spinning, like my body is alive.

Warm enough to feel…anything.

Sometimes, on nights like tonight, watching the gray

shell of my old New York stand still like a ghost in a mist, memories haunt me. I see her face, my mother, looking down, kissing my forehead, and tucking me into bed with three sweet words on her lips. For that moment, a tiny flame flickers in my chest.

A dying fire. Not a burning one. And I wonder when the light will finally fade out. Maybe then I'll get used to the chill.

"Jade!"

I turn at the sound of my name. There is just a shadow, silhouetted by the light of the guardhouse, but I recognize the voice. Brock. One of the boys who was in my training group. One of the many I have since surpassed.

"What?"

"The commander wants to see you." A chorus of low laughter follows his words, but I've grown used to ignoring it.

Stepping out of the dark night, my eyes adjust to the firelight of the guardhouse. Boys sit around a table, playing cards, drinking beer. Their weapons sit by their feet. Bulletproof vests hang on the wall. Some aren't even wearing shoes.

Sloppy.

If the rebellion did attack tonight, I would have to beat them single handedly. But what else is new. There is a reason I prefer the silence of the dark wall, the solitude.

"Where is he?" I sigh.

"The west wall."

I nod and turn back to the door without so much as a goodbye. They won't miss me anyway.

The uneven stones beneath my feet are as familiar as my own limbs, so I jog, letting the sound of my breath fill my ears. To my left lay the last vestiges of what used to be Central Park, the vacant skyscrapers at its boundaries, stretching until everything disappears into thick ebony.

To my right, the complete opposite. The queen's city. Some of us from old Earth call it New New York as a joke. But to those of the magic realm and to most who live here, it is known as Kardenia.

It is a city like I imagine most of Europe must have once looked, if Europe even still exists. Rows and rows of stone houses with chimneys releasing puffs of smoke from burning fireplaces. Not much rhyme or reason to the design, more like roads that interconnect in a large, hard to decipher web. There are stalls for horses, empty merchant carts in the street. And in the center, the castle looms, watching everyone from above.

Still, I've read about the days of old and there are some differences. In the morning, when the streets come alive, there will be bikes zooming. A wood-burning grill might be warming breakfast. The seamstresses will sew with foot pedal machines instead of their hands. Not all of Earth has been forgotten—the gun at my hip is a good reminder of that.

A shadow appears before me, the outline of a man I recognize. The commander. The closest thing to a father I have ever known.

After the earthquake, the queen locked all the children she found in the prisons below the castle, unsure how they would fit into her society. We had too much imagination, I heard her say once. We weren't as afraid as the adults and it made us hard to control.

I was barely down there for a week when the commander came to visit. With slow, purposeful footsteps he walked the length of the long corridor, eyes peering at every little girl huddled against the ground. I was the only one standing, holding onto the bars, staring back at him.

He liked my fight. Said it reminded him of his daughter. The next day, I was pulled from the castle and delivered to his doorstep. There were no hugs, no pats on the head, no pretty dolls waiting for me.

Just as there won't be now.

"Commander Alburn," I call, voice loud against the still night.

"Jade." He turns, hands still locked behind his back. There is no warm recognition in his tone, no smile wrinkling his eyes or puffing his cheeks.

I bow my head, adopting the same rigid stance.

"I was told you needed to speak with me, sir?"

"I do, come with me."

I follow as he spins back around and marches toward

the nearest guardhouse. For a moment, I wonder if people can even spot us from the ground. Black pants. Black long sleeve shirt. Black bulletproof vest. And black boots.

Do we simply fade into the night?

When we enter the guardhouse, the mood is solemn—the men sit at their posts, peering out through slits in the walls. There is no beer, no cards. The way the watch should be, but rarely is. This is the power of the commander.

"Hang up your vest."

My brows scrunch but I heed his order and unbuckle the clips at my side, hanging the heavy garment with others on the wall. There are not enough bulletproof vests for everyone in the guard, so we share, leaving them at the wall for anyone on duty.

To remove it only means one thing. I am being sent home. But why?

"Sir?" I shouldn't ask. I should follow. But I can't help it as the question slips through my lips, out into the open.

"The queen wishes to speak with you in the morning. You are to go home, bathe, and prepare your best dress. Understood?"

"Yes, sir," I automatically reply. But my mind is spinning. The queen?

I have not seen the queen in years, not in close proximity, not since the day I joined the guard. I'm the only

11

girl who has ever done so, the only one who received the queen's blessing.

It was the day I received my black heart, the pin we all wear, the formal sigil of the guard. I was standing in line with a dozen boys, breasts taped down to seem less girly, clothes a size too big so they did not hug my hips. But I fooled no one. And I was not sure if even the commander could convince the guard to accept me, despite my training or maybe because of it.

I was better.

I was a woman.

Those two facts were enough to ostracize me from the pack.

And then with no warning, the queen swept in. Her gown only accentuated her femininity. Her poise only strengthened her power. The men, like a wave, bowed deep.

"My Queen," the commander spoke, voice silencing the murmurs of the guard. "What brings you to our halls?"

"Dear Commander," she said, voice like velvet, smooth and soft, lulling everyone into a trance. "I come to place a pin on the girl who wishes to do the job of a man, to wish her luck and to give her strength. I myself know what sorts of challenges she might face."

The captain holding our pins offered her the plate, and she stepped forward, gracefully selecting a black heart with her delicate fingers. Everyone watched me, eyes fierce. Nothing like this had ever happened before, and I stood still, strong, not breaking my composure.

The pin slid easily into my chest and then her blue eyes met mine, so stark and pale, almost like ice. Her palm came to my face, and I felt it all drain away. The nerves. The doubts. The excitement. Whatever had been there was gone. All of it taken. And I remained still, like a statue, even after she had long disappeared from our halls.

We did not speak then. And I cannot imagine what she would need to say to me now.

"Jade?" The commander's voice flings me back to present day, to the guardhouse, to his command.

I nod my understanding. I will go home. I will prepare. I will not complain.

But before I take my first step, the ground rattles beneath my feet and a boom snaps across the night sky like lightning. All seven of us stop. Our heads twist to the wall, to the darkness of the night, to the source of the noise.

I move first, sprinting through the door.

And then I see it.

A glow in the sky, filtering through the empty streets of old New York, hot white and bubbling red. A cloud. It pops and then only fire remains, fire and the smoke that billows high, blocking out the stars. One of our mines has been detonated.

My hands grip the stone as I peer further, balancing across the edge to get as close as I can. We are all transfixed.

"Rebels." I grin as the word leaves my lips.

"It is just an unlucky animal." The commander overrules me, shuts my words down, and the others nod in agreement.

"Still, shouldn't we take a look?" I lick my lips.

"You will do nothing, Jade, except go home."

I meet his eyes. Both of us are made of stone, hard and unflinching. Time seems to tick between us, stretching, thickening the air. His eyebrow raises and I give in. Dropping my shoulders in defeat, I turn from the scene and shuffle back to the guardhouse.

But as soon as I am hidden behind the stones, my steps grow lighter, swifter, faster. I take the staircase two at a time, racing, until I am on the ground.

I'll get in trouble for this.

I don't care.

My hands fumble with the knots, loosening the reins that tie my horse to her post. In one move, I am on her back. The clicks of her shoes against stone fill my ears, thunderous, loud enough to drift up to the wall.

But by the time shouts rain down on me, I am gone, through the gate. Protests disappear until I am left with only the wind brushing my cheeks and the crunch of grass beneath heavy hooves.

We don't slow until the trees fade and metal takes their place. I am back in the wilds, a concrete jungle more perilous than any forest I can imagine.

But these are my wilds. My home.

A grin spreads across my face, pulls my cheeks until they hurt.

No one can beat me here.

Three

Flash.

It's a good name, a strong name for a horse. And accurate. Like me, she yearns to run free and swift, yearns to break the reins holding her.

But not tonight.

Tonight, my knuckles turn white as they grip the leather keeping her in check. I wish we could run, and in the daylight maybe. But with only the stars to see by, we must move slowly.

Once these vacant streets held cars. Once they were safe to walk on, to ride on. Once they were smooth.

Not anymore.

Debris has claimed this city. Thousands died on the day of the earthquake, the day two worlds merged into one. Buildings toppled, cracked, snapped in two—falling onto one another and causing more destruction. Without the electricity, everyone not under the queen's thrall left, and everyone stuck moved to Kardenia. Abandoned, the city continued crumbling.

We've cleared a few streets as best we could, using carts to carry rock and steel into side alleyways, giving us easy passage for times like these. But who knows what that bomb unsettled and what my horse might step on.

"Shh," I whisper into her alert ear, to soothe and calm her racing pulse.

Orange flickers in the distance, reflecting off not yet shattered windows. A guiding light that calls to me, drawing the two of us closer.

By the location, I know which mine was detonated. We have a few around the city, bombs we managed to put together, buried near different entrances. Two by each bridge and tunnel. From the light ahead, I know the rebels triggered an explosion by the Lincoln Tunnel.

Eighth Avenue is a clear pathway. I've worked on it myself. But the tunnel entrance is not quite aligned with the path, something we did on purpose, to hopefully make the mines look less obvious.

As the fire begins to light my vision, clear enough to make out specific flames in the dark, I slip from Flash's back and tie her to an old post. My sword and crossbow are left in a pile by her feet, too cumbersome for stealth. Better to go the rest of the way on foot, carrying little. Better to stay hidden for as long as possible in case there are survivors.

I wince as my boots crunch on broken glass, impossibly loud to my ear. But the cackle of fire provides the cover I need. When I start to feel the heat of flames against my face, I slip through the open doorway of a building across the street from the tunnel. The door has already fallen in, and the building looks one gust away from collapsing, but it will do for now. Staying low, I creep along the edge of the room, recognizing it as a pharmacy that's been pillaged clean.

Empty shelves have fallen over each other, creating a mound in the center of the room. One ahead of me fell opposite the pack, slipping out the window, a roadblock in my path. Sliding onto my knees, I slither underneath it, careful not to touch any bit of the metal. I don't know how stable the hold is, and the last thing I need is to be pinned.

When I reach the window with the best vantage point, I slowly extend my legs until my eyes have a clear view of the scene before me.

One of the mines has blown, but the second is still intact or I would have heard the blast. Fires burn, dying out with the passage of time. No bodies decorate the ground, no limbs flicker in the light. No paws or claws either. No animals and no humans.

There are no sounds outside of the fire, no moans of pain, and instantly I am on edge. The commander would say it was nothing—that part of a building slipped free and happened to fall on our mine. Nothing more.

But the back of my neck tingles.

Then it is cold.

Metal presses against my skin, the shape of a circle. I recognize the barrel of a gun when I feel one.

"Don't move," a voice whispers, close to my ear. A voice meant to menace, but the ugly tone sounds unnatural, unconvincing.

I should be afraid. I should feel my insides tighten. But they are cool, calm. So hard that I wonder if a bullet would even break my skin.

A second passes and he does nothing. No hand grabs for my shirt. The gun does not press deeper into my skin. I wait for pain, but his touch is gentle. Too gentle for this world.

I react swiftly, throwing my head to the side and reaching my arm back to catch his. I twist my elbow, bending his arm unnaturally until his fingers open and the gun clangs uselessly against the floor. Blindly, I reach down, feeling the tile as I flip myself over. My grip tightens on the handle.

One swing of my arm and we have changed places.

"Don't move," I say, unable to stop my smirk. The gun is aimed at his chest, but I doubt I will use it. Bullets are too precious to waste.

My eyes travel higher, up his neck, past his square jaw, until I meet his eyes. His face holds shock, a little awe. I've seen that look before, during training rounds with the guard. I'm much tougher than I look.

But there is something else.

Something familiar.

The fire behind me floods through the window, illuminating his features and I swear that I've seen them before.

"Are you going to shoot me?" His voice holds a musical quality. It captures me, makes me lose myself for a moment. And suddenly I remember. In a burst, recognition shocks my brain.

The ice-blond hair. The perfect pale skin. The only difference is his eyes, which seem dark as midnight in this light.

It's Queen Deirdre's son. Prince Asher.

"No," I say quickly.

Before my finger accidentally releases a shot, I drop my arm, slipping the clip loose from the gun and sticking the unused bullets in my pocket.

I watch his eyes slide over my shoulder, to the glassless window. He is calculating an escape. But I can't let that happen.

The prince has been missing almost since the day of the earthquake. The only reason I know his face is because every member of the guard must memorize it before they get their pin, before they are officially named a Black Heart. The queen would give anything to have him returned to her.

Maybe even freedom.

"What are you doing here?" I ask, trying to distract him. Killing is easy. It is what I've been trained for, but capturing someone requires a different level of expertise. If I move fast enough, I might be able to use the blunt end of the gun to knock him out. One good blow to the head should do it.

"Touring the city, of course." He smiles, eyes falling back on me. Something stirs inside of them, a sort of deepness I've never seen before.

"What do you think so far?"

"Friendly." He shrugs, unable to completely cover his humor.

If he thinks he can charm his way out of this, he is sorely mistaken. And while he is distracted, I pounce.

He's quicker than I expected. My punch lands on the back of his head, but he has stepped to the side, out of the force of the impact.

While my weight is off balance, he jumps for the window, but I grab his ankle, bringing us both to the ground. Stone or glass, I can't tell which, pokes into my side as we land. Stinging, but not debilitating.

He kicks out. I dodge.

He pulls, using the sill as leverage.

I slide across the floor, fingers sinking deeper into his skin, a relentless vice. He stops to breathe, and I take the moment to yank with all of my strength, bringing him back to the floor with an oomph.

My leg slides over his thighs, trying to secure my hold, but he tosses me to the side with his hands. I fall against the empty shelves.

My eyes go wide as a loud crack fills the shop. Time stops. The ground beneath me shifts. Debris jingles against the floor. I look dumbly at the prince. He has his moment to flee, to watch as the ground swallows me whole from the safety of the window.

Instead, his arm extends forward and I grasp it. One strong wrench and I am flying toward him. The muscles in my shoulder scream as the floor starts disappearing below my feet. But he holds on, pulling me up, and we fall through the open window, cutting ourselves on the way out.

Not a second later, smoke follows us out as the sinkhole fully opens.

Without words, we run. He to the right, me to the left. To safety.

"This way," I yell. He doesn't listen. I can't really blame him. I am, after all, trying to capture him. "There is another mine on that side, come this way."

He stops, eyes glancing to the fire behind him, and sprints toward me. I race until I reach the clean street, the area that the guard cleared—the only area I know is safe in this city.

"Why'd you do that?" My voice is heavy. Thick. I don't recognize the tone. It is new to me.

"You looked like you could use a hand."

I can't tell if the gleam in his eyes is from the fire or from something deeper, something within him. Either way, I let my gaze slip to the cut on his arm, away from his face.

"I would have let you fall," I admit, voice stony.

"I'm not so sure." His voice is quiet. Slow, like time suddenly seems to feel. Long but fragile, thin enough to break.

Voices rise in the distance. Voices I don't recognize.

"You're not alone?" I ask, stupid, but I don't know what else to say. My time has almost run out. If I want to knock him out, I need to do it soon. But my arm hangs limp at my side, rejecting any instructions I give it.

My feet step forward until I am no more than a few inches from his body. He is a little taller than me, but not by much.

He makes no move to run, no move to fight. There's a question in his gaze, a curiosity about what I'll do next.

"If I see you again," my voice is iron, hard with an edge that cuts, "I won't be so generous."

Then I punch him.

He falls, eyes rolling into the back of his head as he drops. One of his friends will find him. I'm sure of it.

My hands are unsteady as I turn around and disappear into the night, never once looking back. They tremble with uncertainty. I have just let it slip away, any chance of freedom, any chance that the queen might release me from her grasp, might reward me.

I have let her son escape.

Squeezing my eyes shut, I bury that truth in the rubble around me, deep in the ground, below the empty subway tracks, shrouded from the light of day.

I hide it.

I forget it.

I forget him.

Four

When I arrive home, the commander is waiting for me.

"Did you have a good time?" He drawls, sipping on a mug likely full of beer. But he is not a drunk—he has too much control for that. Instead, he takes a long sip, slowly, eyes never leaving me, and I know I am in trouble.

There is only one thing that might free me. One lie that I've been working on for the past half an hour as Flash and I returned.

"I think I saw the prince," I mutter.

His eyes go wide. The cup is down and in a blink, he stands before me, gripping my arm. For an older man, he still moves quickly, like a wolf.

"Tell me."

"I went to the mine, it was one of our Lincoln Tunnel bombs," I begin. The best lies, I've found, are the ones that lay just outside the truth. Only slightly fabricated. "I couldn't find any bodies, but I heard voices. I thought someone must have set it off on purpose, so I hid inside a building trying to find the source of the noise. It was a group of men. One of them, I swear, was the prince."

"And?" Disappointment lines his eyes. I know the unsaid words in that question. *And why isn't he here? And why did you fail me? And why did you let him go?*

"The building started to give out underneath me, so I had to run. By the time I circled back around to the group, they were gone."

He wouldn't believe me if I said anything else. He knows me too well—poor odds never would have held me back from a fight. Even if there were five men in the group, I would have taken them on. Ten. I would have charged.

I'm still not sure if he believes me now.

Eyes narrowing, he squeezes just slightly on my arm, trying it seems to peer deep into my heart. We both know he searches in vain.

Completely still, I wait for his mind to come to a decision. I am not nervous. My palms don't sweat, my shoulders do not itch, I feel no need to shift a muscle. There is a constant, solid beat in my chest that does not change.

The one benefit of not being able to feel—it makes lying so much easier.

"Very well." He leans back, satisfied. There is no held breath I need to exhale. No sigh of relief leaves my lips. I've escaped for now. I never expected to be caught anyway. "Go upstairs and prepare for the queen. Dawn is in a few hours, and she will most definitely want to hear this news."

I am released.

Before he adds a punishment to my disobedience, I dash up the stairs. Each creek is familiar, each straining pull of wood. Our house is one of the largest in Kardenia—the queen favors the commander. Three full stories, and my room is at the top, closest to the stars.

I close the door behind me, falling against it. These four walls are my own slice of freedom—here and in the silence of the wall, I am myself. Not just a guard, but also a girl.

All around the room lay trinkets I've scavenged from the old city. My mattress is fluffy and soft, pulled right out of an old shop. Colorful vases line my windowsill, a little collection. Every morning I watch as the sun rises, pulsing through each glass, illuminating my room like a rainbow. A long mirror leans against my wall, framed in wood with yellow paint that has started to chip. I prefer it that way, slightly tainted, not so shiny, not so pretty.

One time during a scavenge in the old city, I happened upon a museum, so I stole a few paintings. They are bright and cheerful, speckled with brilliant flowers and the golden shimmer of the sun. I've hung them over every inch of my walls, so almost no stone is visible. Sometimes I imagine myself in these places. All around the world. Floating through the canals of Venice, pushed by a gondolier. Walking in the gardens of Monet, where petals drift aimlessly on water and trees stretch longingly over lakes. In the tropical forests of South America, surrounded by a world of green, where leaves sometimes surpass humans in size. I wonder if those places even exist anymore. Or if I hold them in my mind, keeping them alive through wishes and dreams alone.

A sigh escapes my lips as I push off from the door and make my way to my armoire, flinging it open. Most of my clothes are black, in total contrast to my room. I've gathered a few pairs of jeans, some warm sweaters, a few woven shirts. But I push them all aside, reaching far back to where my dresses hide. I only have two, both handmade by the seamstresses in town, floor length gowns beaded and embroidered. Far too feminine for my liking.

But the queen, though thrown into a modern world, is very traditional. And if I am going to the palace, I must present myself as a woman and not a member of the guard.

I pull out the forest green silks, opting for the outfit that matches my name and my eyes, and hang it on the door, letting the wrinkles stretch out and flatten. I need to look my best if I am to tell the queen that I saw her son, and I let him get away.

My bed beckons, and I know I should rest, but I find myself gravitating to the window instead. One twist and it flies open, pulled by the wind.

This house is higher than most, so my view extends all the way to the wall and beyond. Sitting in my leather chair, I watch, letting my eyes glaze over. Sleep will escape me, I can already tell. My mind whirls too fast, spinning in circles, going nowhere but never slowing as I recall the events of the night.

I can't remember the last time someone had to save me. Even offered to save me.

That sinkhole would have swallowed me whole, buried me in the ground, if he had not been there. I would be alone in the dark right now if I had survived, buried under rock and steel, bloodied and in pain. Dying a slow death.

Still, I let him go. Does that mean the debt has been paid? Somehow, I don't think it was an even trade.

As the sky begins to glow, a soft yellow hue spreading bluer and brighter with time, I rub my eyes, pushing my tiredness away. Pushing those thoughts away. They were supposed to remain buried in the debris of the city—they were not supposed to follow me home, to haunt my waking hours.

My weary legs stand, shuffle over to my vanity, and I plop down once more. Wrinkles line the bottom of my eyes, dark with lack of sleep.

I start with my hair.

It is long, somewhere between black and brown, almost like it doesn't quite know what it wants to be. Straight near the top then wavy as my fingers travel down. I grab my brush, combing through the knots, wincing as we wage war. When I've won, I twirl it tight, pulling it into an oversized knot atop my head, securing it with a few pins. Not the most magnificent hairdo I've seen, nothing compared to most ladies in the town, but it's the extent of my skills. So it will have to do.

Next, I hesitate before moving onto my face. I look drained, tired. My skin is golden, tanned like honey. A natural glow. But now it looks pallid in the candlelight. When I was little, before the world ended and began anew, the kids at my school used to ask what I was. I remember them teasing me, questioning me. It was only a few months of my life, just before the earthquake, but I still remember. And now I ask the question of myself. My mother never explained. She said she didn't want to label me, that I was a little of everything. Brazilian. Japanese. Irish. Spanish. Words that used to hold so much power but now seem empty.

I dab on some blush, putting life into my cheeks. It is the only form of makeup I've ever bothered to use, perfect for hiding my many sleepless nights. All the other brushes, pencils, and powders I've come across seemed frivolous and unnecessary.

Catching my eyes in the mirror, I pause. My namesake. Jade. Emerald. Two circles that pop. My mother said that before I was born, she wanted to call me Aurelia after her grandmother. But in the hospital, when they placed me as a bundle in her arms, she changed it. My big, beautiful eyes were curious and loving as they looked up at her, and the word just escaped her lips, sounding right.

They are gemstones now. Crystalline. Not soft with love. But I wonder if they still shine with curiosity, at least at times. Probably not.

"Jade!" The commander calls, voice echoing up the staircase. My time is almost up, so I stand, pulling my gaze from the mirror to the dress in the corner. As quickly as I can, I slip my feet through the top, sliding the dress higher up my frame until my arms can sliver through the long sleeves. I fumble with the laces at the back, tightening them as much as possible, and then I delicately knot a bow at the base of my spine.

I own no fine jewelry, so I slip on my black heart pin. It is the only trinket I need. And despite myself, I strap a knife to my inner thigh. But I am stronger that way, more secure, more like myself.

With my flats on, I finally open the door and rush downstairs, meeting the commander in our front parlor. He waits in his formal uniform—exaggerated shoulder pads, golden buttons in two rows down his chest, sword dangling from a fine belt. Fit for the queen.

I wish I could wear similar clothes.

Even though my skirt falls in folds to the floor and my arms are completely covered, leaving only my neck and a small portion of my chest exposed, I squirm, naked somehow.

"Are you ready?"

I nod yes and we exit, making for the painted carriage waiting outside. A footman opens the door and I glide in, resting on red velvet cushions puckered with pearl buttons. The queen sent one of her own carriages to pick us up. I'm uncomfortable, out of place as we bounce on the stone street, jittering around in this box. I wish for the saddled horse I am far more at ease traveling on.

"Are you nervous?" The commander asks.

It's a stupid question, but I don't say that. Instead, I shake my head, and he taps his fingers on his leg, impatient like me. Perhaps he is nervous. But somehow I can't imagine him that way.

"Do you know why the queen wishes to speak with me?" They are close. He often ventures to the palace for meals, meeting in private with the queen. Speaking of the town's security mostly, I'm sure, but perhaps they've discussed me as well. It's a thought I don't wish to dwell on.

"I do," he says, but he catches my eye before I can open my mouth to speak. I hold it shut, waiting, on my best behavior. "But I will not tell you."

I bite my lips together, trapping the protest in my throat.

Silence stretches between us for the rest of the trip. Not necessarily uncomfortable. Neither of us are the sort to babble on just to fill the air. Usually, we both prefer the quiet.

The carriage changes angles, so I am pressed back into my seat, pulled by my own weight. We have reached the hill, the road that circles up and around, winding its way to the gate.

Last time I was here, it was as a prisoner. Now, I come as a guest. The two don't seem very different. Not really.

The carriage pulls to a halt and the door opens. The commander offers his hand and I step down, looking up at the towers looming overhead, spiraling gracefully into the sky.

No guards man this wall. It is whispered that giants hide inside the castle, double the size of any grown man. The queen enlisted them to build her a home grander than any other in the land, taller than any human hands could reach, and once they stepped under her spell, she kept them like pets. Some of the guards who were alive during the war swear they saw them, swear that the giants revealed themselves to fight against the rebels, but no one has seen them since.

I shiver, a light tremble that pulses down to my feet. It's a foreign feeling, one I don't very much enjoy, but a tiny speck of fear leaks into my mind. The only emotion the queen lets us all retain—a bit of dread to keep the people loyal.

The commander ushers me forward, and I follow in step with him as we pass through the gate and walk up a tall staircase to the front door. When we're a few feet away, it opens mysteriously, pulled by someone from the inside, though there are no windows to give our location away.

Below my feet lies a tiled floor, a mosaic of scarlet accented with pearly highlights and onyx shadows. The walls are polished stone, giving the appearance of liquid as the torches cast a glow against the surface. No natural light fills the hall. It is dark, yet soft in the yellow ambiance.

The commander does not stop or turn, he remains straight until the hall opens into a wider room. Vaulted ceilings loom above while sunlight finally filters into view, falling in a beam toward one location.

The throne.

But the carved wooden seat is empty. Its red cushions are fluffed and don't retain the impression of weight. I step forward, past the commander, my shoes scuffling against the tile, wondering if the queen will appear out of thin air, wondering if she sits there now, invisible.

"My sweet Jade."

The voice comes from behind me, slithering across the floor, sliding up my back so it wraps me in a tight cocoon. I am trapped in the notes, stuck in my spot as her words pull me under, suck me in, drown me in magic.

My heart grows colder, smaller, sinking with heaviness until it is lost in a vast sea. The chill extends down my arms, along my spine, to the tips of my toes. My eyes go wide.

Queen Deirdre.

As if controlled by another power, my feet begin to turn.

Five

"Your Majesty."

Even though it comes from my lips, that voice is unrecognizable. Quiet. Meek. Subservient. Not the voice of the girl who defied the commander by riding into the city at midnight. Not the girl who is the best in her training class. Not the girl who has a knife strapped to her thigh, just in case.

The steel presses into my skin, cold, sharp, and I try to hold onto its touch lest I drift away in the power of the queen standing before me. It is my anchor to the heart she controls.

My knees bend into a curtsy and a smile plasters my lips, womanly, like a lady of the court and not a soldier.

"Your Majesty," the commander echoes, bending at his waist into a deep bow.

The queen waits, watches, with hands clasped in front of her hips. As always, red drapes across her narrow frame.

Dark, deep, and in stark contrast to her ivory skin. Rubies decorate the crown nestled in her elaborately braided hair, popping against the icy blonde, alive in the candlelight.

Though I try to look away, my eyes are drawn to hers. An electric shock pricks my chest as her aquamarine irises grab hold, latching on, stilling me, freezing me in place. The dryness starts to burn, to itch, but I cannot blink.

"Welcome," she says and the bond is broken. My lids move rapidly, wetting my eyes, soothing them, and my gaze drifts to the safety of the floor.

"Did you tell her why she was summoned, Commander Alburn?"

The queen's shoes click as she walks farther into the room. My pulse slows to match their steady melodic pace. The effects of being in her presence are starting to wear off—or maybe she is just releasing me, giving my system a break.

"No, Your Majesty. But Jade has news of her own that I feel is pertinent to share first, if Your Majesty will allow it."

She stops walking toward the throne, turning back to us with one brow raised in interest, a small grin on her lips, as though excited by the turn of events.

My throat has gone dry. I swallow.

"Do tell."

The commander steps forward, mouth opening to respond, but she silences him with one flick of her gaze.

"Jade, if it is your news, please share it."

"I…" A cough travels up my neck, followed by a deep breath that shakes my limbs. Stop, I command, yelling at my body. This is not who I am. And I don't believe it is who the queen wishes me to be either.

I steel my veins, turning my body into a knife. The demure girl falls away—I throw her away, out the window, letting that mask break into a thousand tiny pieces as it crashes into the city below.

"I believe I saw Prince Asher in the ruins last night, Your Majesty."

Her brow rises higher, arching into a sharp point. "Continue."

"One of the mines exploded, and I went to investigate. When I arrived, I found a group of men waiting there. I believe they set the mine off on purpose to see how the Black Hearts would respond. Immediately, I recognized Prince Asher from the paintings we have all studied. When I tried to charge, I felt the building shift beneath my feet and needed to flee in safety. By the time I returned, the group had vanished, Your Majesty."

My fingers do not spasm. My lips do not dry. I do not even blink as the lie comes smoothly to my lips. Repeating the story a second time is even easier, even more natural. Part of me almost believes it is the truth, and that my other memory is but a dream, a mirage I made up, a falsehood my mind conceived.

The queen taps her fingers once, then folds them together, decision made.

"Leave us," she orders. The commander twitches, but then salutes in parting. His boots stomp like thunder in the silence.

"There is no need to lie, Jade," she soothes, voice nurturing, caring, like a mother's might be.

Silence is my answer.

"Come," she says, waving her hand as she spins, skirt shuffling against the floor.

I do.

Behind the throne rests an open door, and she leads me through, out onto a stone balcony. The wind is not gentle from this height, and I can feel hair slipping loose from the top of my head, falling from my messy bun. Still, she walks farther, until both of our hands grasp a thick stone railing, smoothly filed so it does not scratch my skin.

"What do you see, Jade?"

My eyes drop below, to the vast city at my feet. Our view points west. To one side are the farmlands, green and lush, extending as far as my eyes can see. To the other, the broken city of New York. The dried up waters of the Hudson River create a path my gaze follows to the ocean, a warm blue compared to the sky.

Shifting up, I take in the massive expanse of air floating above me. I never realized how closely it matches the color of the queen's eyes, as though the clouds might be the only things stopping her from gazing upon the entire world.

"I see Kardenia, Your Majesty." I am not sure what she wishes me to say, but the obviousness of my answer seems almost rude. Still, she smiles as though she expected nothing else.

"Would you like to know what I see?"

"Please, Your Majesty." My fingers tighten on the rail. What does our queen see as she watches over us, barely leaving her towering castle, ruling from a distance?

"I see thousands of people, each one a little beacon of light, calling out to me, pulsing for me. Candles. The city always seems decorated in candlelight, the world even, as though the stars have sunk from the sky to dance in my eyes. I see my magic connecting all of us, connecting all of you to me."

"That sounds beautiful, Your Majesty."

"Does it?" She releases a light breath, a minute laugh. "I thought the same once, I suppose, when my mother described her sight to me. But it is not, it is terrifying, because hiding at the edge of all of that light, is the darkness. The rest of the world is a dangerous place, which is why I hold on to all of you, my children, so tightly. It is to keep you safe, to protect you from the dangers that lay just outside my hold."

"Like the rebels, Your Majesty?" I ask, trying to see the world the way she does, failing. The edges of the horizon are a mystery to me, one I wish more than anything to unveil, to discover with my own eyes. The world waits for me, right in that spot where sea turns to sky, where trees and clouds mold together into an infinite line of light—that is where my soul waits for me.

"Yes, Jade, like the rebels who stole my son, who stole your mother. The rebels who sit at the edge, waiting for the day my power weakens, waiting to destroy us all." The queen turns to me, placing her palm on my arm. Her fingers are icicles against my skin, yet they do not feel cold. "Now, will you speak the truth, Jade? How did you meet my son?"

"I was exploring the bomb site when he held a gun to my head," the words spill out, uncontrollable, because somehow she knows them anyway. Somehow she was with me, watching through my eyes as I let her son go free. No surprise flashes across her face, only satisfaction. "I fought to disarm him, but he was strong, and he threw me away. When I landed, the floor began to give out beneath me, but your son saved my life rather than escape. Once outside, I heard voices, and tried to knock him out, but he was too fast, and I thought it better to make my way back to the wall so I could report the news, rather than allow myself to get captured."

My voice remains even as the last little lie slips out. But I know I cannot tell the queen that I just let her son escape without a fight, without any real reason except that he saved my life. Somehow, that excuse doesn't seem strong enough, not while her gaze weighs on me, shrinking me down until my feet feel stuck in the stone, trapped.

"I know everything that goes on in my kingdom. I know where every human stands, when they move. Their breath surges through my veins. I know when someone enters my realm and when someone leaves, especially my own son. Why did you first lie? Was the truth so hard to speak?"

"I've never lost a fight, Your Majesty—never, until last night."

The queen's gaze softens as she fills in what I did not say. I can only guess what she is thinking, but my mind filters back to the day she placed the black heart pin on my uniform, murmuring about a woman doing the job of a man, and I hope she understands.

I could have used this lie all along. It is closer to the truth, but by saying it aloud I had to admit something—that I had been defeated. I, who have had to prove myself by besting every other man that I've faced, lost.

It is not something I wanted my commander to hear.

Not something I wanted to admit. But now I must.

Silence extends between us, mutual and comfortable, as though there is something unspoken that only we two understand, a bond we somehow share. A tether stretches between our bodies, invisible but growing stronger.

Part of me wishes to grab my knife and chop it in

half. Part of me wishes to leave it alone, to enjoy the connection.

"Good," she says finally. "I asked you here for a reason. Would you like to know what that reason is?" Without waiting for my reply, her arm lifts, pointing out toward the metal wasteland to our left.

"My son waits out there, and I have known it for days. He sides with the rebels against me, and together they plot my downfall. My first instinct was to send a guard to retrieve him, but I have since thought things through. It is not time for him to come home, the pieces have not yet fallen into place, but with your help they may."

"What can I do, Your Majesty?"

"Prince Asher is a good boy, a trusting one. He has always seen the best in people." The words sound as though they should be a good thing, but they spit from her mouth as though vile on her tongue, poisonous. "Take last night, for example. He will see your failure as a kindness, a sort of challenge. And we will use that against him."

As she continues to speak, her face glows with mounting excitement, as though her power surges stronger in her veins. Her eyes are in a far off dream, and I remain silent, watching her mind spin.

"I had a husband once, did you know that? I killed him, just after Asher was born. The man was weak, so easily controlled, so predictable. All the time, trying to save me from myself." She snorts, sneering as her fingers grasp the stone below our fingers. For a moment, I believe it might break beneath her strength, rupturing like all of us have.

"But you understand me, Jade, you understand what it is like to always have doubt whispering in your ear, murmuring that you aren't good enough, urging that the world was right to keep you contained. Like me, it only gives you strength. Like me, it makes you fight harder for what you want."

Her gaze slips to my face, a prickling sensation spreads across my cheek, but I keep my eyes forward, locked on the spot I wish to be—the edge of the world.

"I wanted to be queen, and here I am. And I know what you want, Jade, I see the yearning in your eyes." The queen leans in, her breath like a winter's breeze tickling my skin. My muscles tighten, hard as rock so I do not flinch.

"Freedom," she whispers.

Freedom.

The idea flashes before my eyes, a signal that blinds, just out of reach.

Her fingers shift, landing gently on top of mine, which now clutch the railing. Power surges up my arm, stinging, bringing pain-filled tears to my eyes as it travels up to encase my heart.

But it is not cold, it is warm, like lava that burns my skin, melts my insides away. For a moment, I see the stars, moving, twinkling, dancing all along the ground. I feel everyone and everything in Kardenia.

There are children playing in the street, and I bubble with their laughter. A guard on the wall is drunk, passed out while still in uniform. The slow beat of his heart thrums in my head. The commander waits out of sight, but his insides are knotted tight in curiosity. And far off in the distance, people are walking and talking, muffled so that I cannot hear, but their pulses swell in my veins.

My heart expands, stretching wider than this kingdom, growing with my awareness. The world is at my fingertips, at my command, as though I can just reach out and take it, control it, experience it.

The queen releases me and the awareness vanishes.

Gone.

My eyes are left blind, spotted. My senses are dull. I feel nothing, empty without the souls of a thousand people funneling through my body.

"You can have your freedom, Jade, I promise. But first, you must let my son capture you. You must travel with him to the rebel camp. You must teach him to trust you. And then you must bring him here, to me, unharmed."

I understand what she is asking. It would be easier to send a team to capture the prince. It would be simpler to wait for him to return with the rebels at his back. But the queen knows that, and it is not what she wants.

When I was a child, the queen stole my heart. But now she wants me to let it go willingly, to forget I ever had one in the first place.

One betrayal and I can have my freedom.

Is she testing me?

Is she testing her son?

I do not know, and though I should, I cannot bring myself to care. There is more going on here than I realize, more to this game than I can see with my limited perspective. How do I compare to a queen who has the eyes of a million people? How can I beat her?

The answer is simple.

I cannot.

The picture of freedom dances before my eyes, like the paintings decorating my bedroom, framing the far off horizon. I see the world I have studied in books, the cities I yearn to explore, and it is within my reach. Finally.

"I will do what you ask, Your Majesty." I turn to meet her calculating gaze, her wide smile.

"I know."

With those two words, my prayer of freedom disappears and in its place, imaginary shackles bind my wrists, chain me to the queen, ensnare me.

The key disappears into the silver highlights of her eyes. My throat closes as the single emotion I am allowed to feel burns my chest.

Fear.

Dread.

And my thoughts whisper one question into my ear.

What have I done?

Six

"Jade, where are you going?" Brock calls. I ignore him, glancing over my shoulder to the dusty gray building that has caught my eye.

The library.

My fingers itch to explore all of the pages I have left untouched, to run along the smooth paper edges, to lose myself in those halls.

The six of us are on a scavenging mission beyond the wall, in the old city. Brock and the others believe we have been sent to look for medical supplies—pills, sterilizing wipes, Band-Aids—all things that we have lost the ability to produce but can still find out here. Most of the pharmacies and hospitals have been emptied, but sometimes we strike gold in apartment buildings that were left in a hurry.

The truth? This is my mission and mine alone. I am to separate myself from the group, lure the prince out, and allow him to capture me.

Now seems as good a time as any.

"I'll find you guys in a little while," I yell to the boys, who have all stopped walking to stare back at me. The black uniforms almost look funny in the daylight, so stark against the debris, which is coated in a fine layer of powder, muting all the colors around us. Brock rolls his eyes, leading the other boys back around to continue the way they were going. They visibly slacken, losing their formal stances, smiling, slapping one another on the back as they walk away with jokes on their lips.

No protest or shout of safekeeping filters back to me, but I'm not surprised. We always leave the city as a group, and once safely beyond the sight of the wall, I always split off. Nothing unusual. In fact, I bet they wonder why I took so long today.

I ask myself the same question.

Delay is not something I'm used to. I prefer to charge, racing forward without a second thought, despite overwhelming odds or orders to the contrary. But today, my mind is in knots. From the outside, my demeanor looks calm and stoic, but inside my thoughts are in turmoil.

Everything starts today. And though I will do anything for my freedom, I wonder if this is a mission I can truly pull off. My heart is hard. It does not weaken in empathy for the prince I will deceive. It does not ache with the morality of my actions. No, my heart is not the problem.

Failure.

That is the squirmy idea wriggling around my insides, pausing my movement. I had never failed at anything until I met this prince, and I do not want to experience that again. Especially not when my freedom is truly on the line, when it is so close, closer really than I ever dreamed.

I cannot fail if I never try.

But that in itself would be a failure.

I sigh and step onward, toward the building that before caught my attention, finally moving me into action. The New York Public Library. It is a short building, buried among skyscrapers, but somehow imposing, built with stone and not metal, more lasting. The entrance is framed by unbending columns and is guarded by two stone lions—ones I used to dream would come alive and whisk me away.

I have no such notions now. Magic is not my friend. Magic will never come and save me.

I make my way slowly up the steps, leading to the archway sheltering the front doors. Once inside, I notice familiar footsteps along the ground, unsettling the dirt. Boot shaped grooves cut into the dust, revealing the hidden beauty of the floor below. They are my own prints, from the last time I visited.

To the guard, a library is useless. It houses no clothes for the people. No medicines. No food supplies. None of our former comforts.

But it houses something else—knowledge. A tool I have found more useful than all the others.

I follow the familiar path of my steps, putting a new layer of prints onto the ground, a trail for the prince to pursue.

There are rooms here that I have not visited, filled with pages of fake lives and make-believe stories, worlds imagined and conceived on paper. Works that hope to reveal the true nature of human struggle, the motivations of passion, the joy of love, the sting of hatred, the ache of loneliness. I find it all useless, beyond the scope of my mind, beyond the reach of my cold heart.

Perhaps in a different life, I would have been able to lose myself in all of those emotionally taut words, but in this life, I crave facts, information. And I make my way to my favorite room, where encyclopedias line the walls and textbooks rest waiting for students to turn their pages, settling on me instead.

The stone hallways are quiet and my steps echo from wall to wall, until I stop in a doorway, breathing for a moment, wondering if this will be the last time my eyes behold this scene.

The reading room, my favorite room. It was grand once, I imagine, clean and sparkling, illuminated by the stained-glass windows lining the walls. Now it is muted. The windows are shattered, letting a breeze stir stale air. The once majestic chandeliers lay mostly broken on the floor, bulbs in shards. A few still hang, pulsing eerily from the touch of invisible hands. Desks line the floor. Chairs are turned over. Surfaces rest covered in gray ash. And the ceiling, made of carved wood and painted with clouds, actually has a hole, broken by the steel beam impaled in the floor.

But the books still rest peacefully. Most of the shelves survived the earthquake because they were nailed to the walls. The books crashed to the ground, but as I read them, I place them back in their spots. Most have a home now. They gently rest against one another, old friends happy to be back where they belong.

Warped pages, wet from rain, dried in the summer heat, have made the books thicker. Tougher. And I like to think, more resilient.

Gently I remove my crossbow from my back, leaving it to rest on a tabletop. My vest goes next. But I leave the gun strapped to my thigh, and the sword resting at my hip. I want the prince to catch me unaware, but I can't be too obvious.

I am not even sure he was looking as I left my group, but there was a sensation, a tingling around my spine whispering that I was being watched. The prickle is still there, pinching my neck, making my hairs stand on end. If he is not here, he is coming. I'm sure of it.

Casually, without any sign of worry, I walk along the edges of the room, letting my fingers bump along the shelves, running over the leather-bound covers. After I discovered the museum and stole those paintings for my bedroom, I came to the library. I knew that the gardens, the cities, the architecture depicted within those frames were based on someplace real. And I discovered a series of books all about the history of art from around the world. I found my paintings, my places, my dreams, and countless other destinations I promise to one day explore.

As my fingers land on a deep maroon spine highlighted with gold lettering, I stop. But the sound of feet still rings in my ears, soft, growing louder. They should have removed their shoes, I smirk, socks are much more conducive to sneaking.

Pulling on the book, I drop it loudly on the tabletop next to me, sitting so my back is facing the door, and I cannot see the entrance. That is the last gift I will give them. From here, my fight becomes real.

I slowly open it, letting ridged pages crackle against one another, but I am not paying attention to my books any longer. They are lost to me as the boots stop clicking. And then a soft, one, two, one, two. The prince is greeting me alone. I shake my head, gritting my teeth in annoyance. That was not part of the plan.

The walking stops.

I pause.

The air thickens, and I force my muscles to stay still, not to turn, not to move. I will give nothing away. I wait as the silence stretches, wondering what he thinks, wondering why he does not take the advantage.

"I'll admit, I didn't take you for a scholar," a deep voice calls from behind me. Not overly loud, but in this cavernous room, the volume grows, bouncing from ceiling to floor.

I sit tall, as though shocked free from my reverie, and stand, hand immediately gripping my gun. My head whips around until my eyes land on his relaxed pose, arms folded over one another, knee bent. A smile dances across his lips.

"I'll admit, I didn't take you for an idiot," I reply, releasing my weapon and adopting my own relaxed stance, hip cocked to the side, hands on my waist. "Well, that's not entirely true. But I did warn you what would happen if I saw you again."

The prince only shrugs, stepping forward. His gaze slips behind me, to the desk at my back. "What are you reading?"

"The encyclopedia," I answer. There is no need to lie. But still, I ask myself if this is why he followed me around? Friendly banter?

"Fascinating." He lets out a breath, widening his eyes and raising his eyebrows, clearly trying not to laugh. One of his cheeks is bruised a deep blue from my fist. I can easily make the other one match, in fact, my fingers clench, ready to remove the smirk on his lips.

"Do you have a better suggestion?"

"Than the encyclopedia?" He looks around, eyes wandering the walls before settling back on me. "Maybe not in this room, but definitely yes."

"What?"

"I'll tell you someday," he teases, and I realize how close I've allowed him to walk. The prince is within a few feet of my body, close enough that our swords could dance, maybe even close enough that our fingers could touch.

In the light of day, he looks different. The angles on his face are not as harsh as the queen's. They are softer, subtler. Cheekbones that roll into his jaw, lips that are full, a nose that rounds just slightly at the tip. Skin still pale, hair still blonde, but his eyes look newer, brighter, deeper still.

Indigo.

But I know that can't be right. Yet, as I meet his gaze, his irises shine back, dark as midnight, sparkling with stars, streaked with plum highlights. An entire galaxy seems alive in his eyes.

"Why are you here?" I try to step back, but my thigh hits the table, unable to move any farther.

"Because you're such a brilliant conversationalist, obviously." One corner of his lip lifts and his eyes twinkle, waiting for my reply.

But I've had enough.

My foot reacts first, rising into a kick, slamming into his stomach. The prince doubles over, stepping backward, and I continue to charge, shoving against his shoulders so he falls fully to the floor, knocking into a table on the way down.

I land on his chest, pressing the end of my gun against his head.

"I know you won't kill me," he challenges.

"Try me," I hiss, leaning forward, leaving my side open for an attack. But he doesn't punch, he doesn't move, just keeps staring into my eyes as though searching for something.

"You don't have it in you."

I press the metal further into his forehead, causing an indent. "I've killed a man before."

It's a lie, but not by much, and my voice does not falter as I speak it. A year ago, a rebel attacked my group while we were scavenging for medical supplies. I shot him. The bullet landed on his shoulder, narrowly missing his heart, but he lived. He works as a baker now. Barely even bats an eyelash when I buy my bread. I don't think he even remembers who I am.

The prince's brows twitch, confused, and I know instantly that the queen was right, that her plan will work. He believed me to be soft, a kindred spirit since I let him go free. Now he is unsure, but still curious—interest still lightens his eyes.

Then the fist I've been waiting for nails my gut, flipping me from his chest and across the floor. I release the gun, letting it skid over the tiles, hoping it doesn't look like I dropped it on purpose.

We both stand, and he edges to where the gun slowed

to a stop, cutting off my resource like I hoped he would. I spring the opposite way, sprinting to the center of the room, away from the desks to an open area, and I pull out my sword.

He follows, slow, eyeing me warily as he slides his own sword free.

I move left.

He follows.

Right. Right. Left. Left. Over and over as we circle each other, neither gaining the advantage, neither attacking. But I grow tired of this game quickly, and I strike, swinging my blade in a wide arc that should be easy enough to block.

He does. A ring echoes across the room, metal on metal, the scrape of sharp edges testing one another. Our swords meet again, singing as we clash over and over, contorting our bodies to escape and parry. The dance makes my muscles burn with life. I find myself grinning, breathing heavy, stretching body parts that I haven't used in a while, finally facing a foe who is my match.

But not quite my match. I am more skilled. He is stronger. With every minute, my arms lose a little fight, my blocks grow a little softer, my attacks a little slower. His remain steady, unflinching.

So I play dirty, dropping to the ground while his sword swings overhead, using my leg to swipe at his feet, knocking him over once more. As he falls, I roll over his sword arm, placing my blade across his throat.

Our chests heave together, pressing and pulling against one another. Pink flushes his cheeks, enlivening his features, making his eyes seem darker, fuller. The distance between our faces is small, but time seems to stretch between it, expansive, vast.

"You're right," I say, relaxing my arm, "I don't have it in me."

I don't know if that's true or if I say it as a ploy to gain his trust. But I'm not sure I want to know. So I stand, rolling free from his chest while I drop my blade, breathing easier with the distance, letting the breeze cool the sweat from my brow.

He doesn't move from the floor, but his gaze shifts.

My eyes wander to the doorway.

We have visitors.

Four men watch on. They are older, not as fit, bulging slightly at the waist. Amusement is clear on their faces, as though the prince and I were putting on a show.

Well, we'll see how they like this.

In one leap, I am standing on top of a table. Before they can react, I am running, jumping from desk to desk toward the back of the room. Their feet pound in pursuit, but I have the advantage. I know this room inside and out.

As I reach the end of the row, I jump, hands gripping for the iron bars of the railing a few feet above my head. There is a second-floor balcony lining the edge of the room, and it would mean my escape.

My hands fasten around metal and I hang on, two choices flashing before my eyes.

I've made this jump before, practicing, leaping for fun just to see if I could—and I can. The men would never make it, too old and out of shape, but the prince might. Either way, I would have time on him, and I know where the exits lead, which halls to travel. I would lose him in the maze of this building, and then I would return to the queen, defiant, letting her know that she did not own me. But in that defiance, I would be stuck, trapped forever in her thrall. The places in my paintings would melt away, disappearing even from my dreams.

Or I can hang here, let their hands pull me to the ground, let them capture me and hold me prisoner, following the queen's plans perfectly. In the end, I would gain my liberty, but she would still own me forever. Though I would be free to wander the world, I would never fully be free from her or the choice she forced me to make.

Indecision stills me. Stalls me.

Hands grip my ankles, and I know it is too late. One yank and I am on the ground, tangled in beefy arms that seem to appear from nowhere as they hold me still, bind my wrists, my ankles, tie a cloth over my eyes. I am blind.

In the darkness, a voice whispers, "I'm sorry."

Pain explodes in my head, zipping down my back until my entire body burns. And then it disappears.

I disappear.

Seven

When I wake, darkness greets me. Black stripes crisscross my vision, thin and mildly translucent, almost like thread. Like a blindfold, I realize as a trickle of boastful conversation filters into my ear, too loud for my pounding head to handle.

My body wriggles, aching for freedom, but I quickly realize my hands are bound tightly behind my back and my feet, too, are strapped together.

The noise travels from behind me, so I use my strength to flip my body, rolling over my hands, biting my lips to keep from crying out at the pain of straining already spent muscles. Fire flickers dully into view, bringing my eyes slowly back to life. A shadow passes quickly in front of the fire, and the crunch of feet on leaves trickles into my ear.

My body goes completely still.

Fingers slip into my hair as hands convene, twisting at the back of my head until the cloth falls free. I blink rapidly, fighting the sting of sudden brightness, fire blazing before my face.

Four men sit around the flames, all eyes on me while they sit quietly and pick at the bones in their hands. The smell of roasted bird fills my nose, causing a grumble to rise in my stomach, loud and painful. I ignore it, surveying the scene as fast as I can. We are surrounded by trees, far from the city and completely alone. Each man sits with a gun and knife strapped to his waist. A large rifle leans against a tree behind them. There is probably another hidden in the grass by their feet.

If I could cut my binds, I would likely be able to slip free into the night. I doubt they would waste bullets following after me—an injured prisoner is much more difficult to deal with. Either way, I should probably try to escape. It would be suspicious to be too complacent, to seem too willing to be caught.

A fifth man is behind me, and I assume it is the prince. His boots shuffle against the ground and warm fingers touch my wrists, skin on skin, but then they pause.

"Are you going to run if I untie your hands?" His voice is smooth like velvet, washing over me. The same commanding voice of the queen, somehow empowered.

Like the queen, my gut tells me that I cannot lie to him. That he would see through me. Somehow, he would know. So I tell the truth. "Yes."

His hands abandon the bare skin of my wrists, finding my shoulders instead. Cradling me, he lifts my upper half from the ground, using his strength to help me sit upright.

"I appreciate your honesty," he says and steps into view, crouching down to my eye level. I meet his penetrating gaze.

"Would you have believed me if I said no?"

The only reply I receive is a deep grin, and then he stands, walking close to the fire and grabbing a plate of food.

"Do you like chicken?"

"Do I have a choice?"

"I suppose not."

"Then, yes."

His tone sounds amused, but I keep my face blank as he comes back to sit at my side. He cuts through the meat with a knife and fork, teasing me with the possibility of escape if I could just slip that blade free without his realizing.

I look up and he is watching me, eyes reflecting the fire, gaze intrigued as he puts the plate on the opposite side of his body, setting the knife down a full three feet from my eager hands.

The fork rises to my lips and I bite, eyes popping wide as the flavors explode behind my lips.

"Do you know who we are?" He asks, hands back to work on feeding me dinner. Another slice of chicken rises to my mouth and I accept it eagerly, savoring the spicy taste before I respond.

"Rebels."

He pauses, trying to catch my eye, but I keep my glance down, focused on the food. I will not reveal that I know his identity, not so soon, not until I can use it to my advantage. For now, they are five rebels, five enemies I would love nothing more than to destroy.

The prince sighs. "I suppose that's how you would think of us, but I don't fault you. The queen's power is strong."

"What would you know about it?" I peer sideways, but he ignores me, not at all fazed by the question.

"My name is Asher," he continues, and I swallow quickly, surprised that he tells me his real name. Perhaps he doesn't realize that the name Asher is well known through Kardenia, very much wanted.

Attention back on the fire, Asher points to the first man on the left, who continues to stuff himself, face greasy with chicken juice. "That's Toby." He shifts to the right, to a man who sits with his hand at his waist, guarding his knife with nimble fingers. "That's Dave." He moves to the next man, who is broad and wide, with a midsection that pooches just slightly over his pants. A smile waits for me on his lips, almost kind. "That's Joe." Finally, his finger lands on the last man, who does not watch me but instead turns a stick, rotating the bird roasting in the fire. "And that's Al."

There is a pause, stretching into tense silence. I know what they wait for, but I feel like being difficult.

"And you are?" Asher finally asks, putting my now empty plate back on the ground. His body inches farther away from mine, leaving the air empty, hollow.

"Your captive," I say, swallowing the last remains of my dinner.

The prince nods, as though he expected nothing different from my response. Their gazes fall to the blindfold at my feet, but I don't want darkness anymore, so I know I must continue the conversation. I must try to be nice, no matter how difficult that may be.

"Where are we?" I ask. "Where are you taking me?"

"We left the city last night," the prince begins, and as he speaks, the four other men in the group lose interest, returning to their dinners. I wonder if the prince is truly part of them, or if he feels alone, surrounded by men who were born in a different world than he. The rebels are all from the original Earth—at least I assume so. No one from the magic realm has ever been able to leave Kardenia or the queen, no one except for the prince who sits before me.

Still, his face gives no impression of sadness. It is like happiness perpetually floats around him. A smile always graces his lips, a fire always seems alive in the dark nebula of his eyes.

He leans back to rest on his forearms, casual while he continues. "And traveled all day today before you awoke. I believe we are in a place you would know as New Jersey, traveling west toward our base, which happens to be where we're taking you."

"Why?"

"Because I have a theory I'm trying to work out," he answers, but the words seem more for himself because I don't understand the meaning behind them.

"And why let me know the way?"

The prince shrugs. "We'll keep you mostly drugged until we arrive, though I told the others it's not necessary. No one in Kardenia could travel there willingly—it's too far removed from the queen's power, she would never allow it. Even if you escaped, you could never find it again."

"How can you be sure?" I ask, curious. I've never spoken to anyone so freely about the magic before, especially no one so knowledgeable.

Asher meets my gaze, eyes full, brows downcast, lids crinkled, like he knows my soul and is sorry for it. "I was born in Kardenia, so I know the effects of the queen's thrall when I see them. And you've fallen deeper than most."

"How can you tell?"

He leans closer, so I can almost feel his breath on my cheek while he thinks. I do not back away, I hardly move as he assesses me.

"You don't flinch," he starts, and he is right. No tremor pulses down my veins. Nothing moves my muscles. The prince takes that as a sign to continue, and his gaze travels with his words, searching me for more secrets. "Your breath is calm and even despite your situation. Your gaze never leaves a cool level of calculating, looking for weakness, looking for openings to escape. Your speaking tone never changes. It doesn't rise in surprise, lower in remorse, or deepen in anger. Even now, you watch on, silent as I speak ill of you, raising no words to defend yourself. I've barely seen you smile, which I guess is understandable given the situation, but I also haven't seen your fists clench or your jaw square with fury."

He pauses and I remain as I am, watching, quiet, immobile on the ground. The prince lounges, but his tone has gained a fullness I am not used to. His throat seems tight. "But mostly, it is the questions you've asked. Not a single worry has slipped through your lips, no fear that someone might miss you at home, might come looking for you. No commanding threat that a loved one will seek revenge, because loved ones don't really exist in Kardenia, not as I've come to realize they can."

"And yet," he says, turning, flipping onto his side so it is obvious I have his full attention. My gaze does not shift from the fire, but my concentration has faltered slightly, drawn in by his words. "You didn't capture me when you had the chance. You let me go. So maybe you're not in as deep as it might seem."

I know this is an opening I should take advantage of, a moment where I can gain his trust like the queen wants, but those words will not come. They flicker in the firelight, waiting to be said, waiting for my lips to steal them from the flames.

I could denounce the queen and it might sound real. I could say I allowed myself to get captured so I might escape her hold. I could admit I needed to force someone to drag me away, so I might finally be free.

I could say all of those things to make this trusting boy trust me.

But I say none of them.

Instead, I look up at the leaves hanging overhead, the darkest shade of evergreen, swaying so the sky flickers just beyond, and I say one word.

"Jade."

"What?" Asher shifts his weight. I've caught him off guard—I can tell by the way his body jerks back to face me. I've pulled him from his thoughts, likely similar to mine, ruminations on the queen neither of us can escape.

"My name," I repeat softly. "My name is Jade."

A moment passes between us, brief, but I know it is significant. My heart twinges uncomfortably, a feeling I haven't experienced before, almost as if something has tugged on it, urging it to life.

"Thank you," Asher says, breaking the bond and I curl into my knees, stone once more.

He gets up and walks back to the four other men, expression coming alive as he leaves me on my own. They laugh as he sits and tells a joke, casting a jovial bubble over the group while I rest cold on the outside.

But my attention is on what the prince left behind. A knife sits three feet away and I could inch my way over, but I sense this is a test. He is too careful to leave such an opening by chance.

I'm not sure what Asher is testing. My loyalty to the queen? My loyalty to him?

But it is not a question of loyalty, not for me. It is a question of freedom. If I use the knife, I have no doubt of my ability to escape. But I would be running back to the past, back to what I know, back to a life that never changes, never excites.

But if I leave it, I move forward into the unknown. What will happen when we pass beyond the threshold of the queen's thrall? She seemed to think the bond would not break. The prince seems to think otherwise. And I do not know. But I am willing to find out, willing to try.

So before I can change my mind, I fall on my side, to the direction opposite the knife, as though laying down for sleep. I wince as my head knocks against the dirt, further bruising an already sore wound, but my chest feels light.

I look back to the fire and realize the prince's eyes never left mine. The hint of a smile graces his cheeks, and I know he knows my choice. I also know I've passed his test.

He walks back over, a cup in hand, and eases down next to me.

"Drink this," he whispers as he helps raise my head from the ground. The liquid burns as it travels down my throat, but I do not cough as the fire reaches my stomach.

"Drugs?" I ask, but I already know the truth. My lips feel fat and my eyes begin to blur, almost masking his affirmative nod.

The flames expand, tingling down my arms and legs until I am numb from the heat—numb in a different way than I ever have been before. The stars seem brighter, the trees expand and spread across the sky, warping as my mind begins to fade away.

"Can I tell you a secret?" The prince leans down. His pale skin glows luminescent in the firelight, brighter now, almost blinding to my eyes. His fingers brush my upper arm, blazing hot, but I do not flinch. I cannot move. My body is bound, my mind floats up with stars, far away.

"I knew you wouldn't take the knife," he murmurs, voice like a lullaby that releases me, frees me until I am drifting in the beyond.

And then bright dreams take hold.

Eight

I don't know how long the fever continues.

All I know is that the world has become a series of flickering pictures I do not fully understand. Dreams that fold in and out of each other, interrupted by a reality that seems imaginary. I see my mother watching over me, brushing my hair from my sweaty forehead, kissing me goodnight. I see the queen watching me with victory in her eyes, triumphant smile on her lips. I see the commander looking on stoically as I am given special honors. I see the world through free eyes, I see my paintings come to life, I see an endless horizon waiting for me.

And then there are times when I see the prince. His eyes dark and deep with concern, skin like moonlight. He says words I do not hear, cannot register. He feeds me, forces liquid down my throat and food into my empty stomach.

Beyond him, the stars sparkle.

Even now, my eyes flicker, coming to wakefulness but I do not know if this is yet another dream or if my sickness is finally over.

The darkness behind my lids is almost comforting. There is a nothingness that feels safe, soothing compared to the madness I've been living these past few days. Weeks? I don't know.

Without opening my eyes, I groan and stretch my muscles. They ache too much for this to be anything but real. My arms extend overhead, and my fingers hit stone. Smooth stone. Too flat to be natural.

I sit up, forcing my lightheadedness aside, and realize there are cushions below me. Perhaps a mattress.

"You should rest," a familiar voice says. Slowly, dropping my weary head into my palms, I open my eyes toward the sound.

The prince sits next to me in a lush chair, expression full of concern, but I am too curious to bother responding. Instead, my eyes wander.

Below us, a woven rug lines a concrete floor. I am sitting in a bed, body kept warm by thick blankets decorated with bright flowers that are far too feminine for my taste. A door rests closed beyond the foot of the mattress, a door and not bars. But still, I will not fool myself. This is prison—pretty, but nonetheless a cell.

There are no windows, I realize, even though curtains hang along the walls, covering up dull gray stone—flat like what I felt behind me. A subtle blue glow fills the room, unnatural, not from a fire.

I gasp.

It's not possible.

My hand rises to cover my mouth, and my feet begin to work on their own. Tired legs force me to stand, slip from the bed, and make their way to the center of the room. I do not stop until I am directly below the source of the light, basking in its glow.

A light bulb.

Electricity.

It's different from the round globes I remember. This glass is twisted into an oval, emitting a cool tone.

I swallow a shaky breath as my hands tremble, reaching up.

"I wouldn't..."

But I ignore Asher. I need to feel it. To touch it. To make sure it is real.

My fingers barely brush the glass and it burns, stinging fire into my skin. I rest there for a second, embracing the heat, before snatching my hand back. My eyes have started to go blind from staring so directly at the source, but I am entranced. I cannot look away.

"Pretty cool, right? Scared the crap out of me the first time I saw a light bulb."

The words pull me in and I switch my gaze, staring now at the prince. "How? When?"

The grin on his face widens at my surprise, and he leans forward, animated. "Welcome to life outside of Queen Deirdre's realm. I don't think they ever lost the electricity out here. It's been on for as long as I can remember."

"Where are we?" I stumble back, unsteady, memories flashing before my eyes. Memories of my cityscape brightly lit against a black sky, of my books illuminated by the pink lamp on my nightstand, of my mother's face in a warm yellow glow just before she kissed me goodnight.

My legs hit the bed and my weight falls back, landing with an oomph on the mattress as my mind spins.

"Far enough away that the queen's magic can't touch us."

I meet his gaze, pit clumping in my stomach. The prince might think that, but even if the lights work, I am never free. I feel her still, ice in my veins, watching me.

He keeps talking, not at all discouraged by my silence. "We're in the rebel base, as you would call it. It's an underground complex." His thumb points over his shoulder at the bare wall. "No windows. There's an old town above us, abandoned buildings that act as a good cover to keep us a secret. Each roof has solar panels that trap the sun and turn the energy into the electricity that powers this place." He shrugs. "I don't much understand it, but it's something like that, I think."

I nod. My mouth is still too dry for words, but I remember reading something about that in my books, different forms of energy—wind, solar, coal. Others still. The information is trickling back into awareness.

The silence is broken as the prince laughs suddenly, a barking sound that escapes his lips against his will.

"I'm sorry," he says between chuckles, "but if you could see your face right now." He shakes his head, falling back into the chair, watching me, mirthful. "Flip the switch, I dare you."

I follow the flick of his eyes toward the door and see a small box on the wall. In its center rests a circular button. Hesitant, I look back at him, encouraged by his confidence. And then I stand, walking across the space until my fingers rests on the plastic. I lick my lips. Swallow.

Click.

The darkness is immediate and thick. The prince, the walls, the room. All of it disappears until I almost wonder if I am back in the fever dreams. Except I look up, watching as the light bulb slowly continues to fade out. The ceiling has a slight blue glow. It is the only thing I can see in this forever night, but even that begins to putter out. The halo shrinks, closing in, slipping through my fingers.

Click.

The light bursts back to life, shocking my eyes, but with it, something stirs inside me. A tingle scatters down my limbs as a grin comes to my face, an emotion I can't place. Mild warmth fills my bones, fighting against the chill. It feels foreign, as unnatural as the lights.

Click.

Darkness again.

Click.

Bright lights shine on.

Click.

Click.

Click.

I continue until my eyes begin to hurt, but my laughter fills the room, mixing with the prince, making a sort of music I thought had been lost to me forever.

On.

The prince sits in his chair, doubled over.

Off.

He disappears.

On.

Asher is standing now, eyes glowing like the light bulb above our heads, magical.

Off.

He is gone.

On.

He is closer, only a few feet away, arms on either side to keep his balance in this ever-changing atmosphere.

Off.

I breathe deeply, wondering what sight will greet my eyes next.

On.

Asher is right next to me, hand coming on top of mine, warm, stopping me from turning the lights off again. My throat closes, and I am trapped by his eyes, held captive by the stars that glow there. We both pause. But somehow it seems like we're conversing, as though the touch of our skin is communicating in a way that words cannot.

I break the moment, stepping back, pulling my hand free, letting my insides freeze over once more. I don't stop until I am back at the bed, far away, enough distance between us for my head to stop spinning.

He is the sun and now my limbs grow cold again. Winter seeps into my skin, but I am more comfortable this way, more like myself, more like the Jade I have come to know. I'm not sure whom that girl was, playing, smiling, laughing.

It was not me.

I am stoic, controlled, hard.

I am not the girl who creates music. I am the one who silences it.

My expression clears as my facial features fall into their normal state, relaxed and empty. I clench my fists, open them, close them again.

Finally, I look back to the switch.

Asher is watching me. A frown bends his face, twists it in a way I know is unnatural to him.

I force myself not to care.

He coughs, slipping his weight from the wall, clearing

his features so I cannot read them. But he stays by the door, cautious.

"I should probably get back to work." He sighs, shrugging his shoulders and slipping his hands into the worn pockets of his jeans.

"Okay. Go ahead," I say. My tone is ambivalent, uncaring.

"Someone will bring you dinner and some snacks, and I'll be back to check on you…" He trails off, waiting.

"Okay."

He nods to himself, a subtle move. His fingers wrap around the door handle, and I hold my breath, stilling myself, biting back a protest.

He turns his back on me, walking out the door.

But then he stops, twisting back around.

"Oh, one more thing," Asher's voice is soft. His eyes do not meet mine but glance toward the corner of the room. "I brought you some books. Way better than encyclopedias."

And then he is gone.

I stare at the wooden panel until my heart slows to a steady beat, its normal melodic pace. Then I stand, test the handle, feel no surprise when the knob does not budge. I am trapped, stuck. The rebels do not trust me.

Smart.

Even I do not trust me.

With a sigh, I push off from the door and step to the

small stack of books in the corner. Without a doubt, they are the sort to contain made up stories filled with make-believe characters. Small, with bindings that have creases from being flipped through so many times, the shape is completely different from the heavy volumes I'm used to.

I sit down, folding my legs over one another, as I grab the first book. The cover holds the image of a man dressed entirely in dark clothes, almost as though he were a Black Heart, and hanging on his arm is woman in a pink flowing gown. They seem lost in the woods. She seems in need of rescuing. I read the title, *The Princess Bride*, and put it aside for later. I am no princess, and I am not interested in a damsel in distress.

The next depicts a boy dressed in green, seemingly flying through the air, followed by other children. A girl and two boys maybe. *Peter Pan*, I read. But I have no interest in reading about more magic.

After that, a title called *Twelfth Night*. I flip it open, but the language confounds my mind, so I put it aside until a time when I can force myself into such concentration. Right now, I'm distracted. Half of my thoughts wander with the prince, down these halls and away from me, useless.

I continue reading titles. *Pride and Prejudice. The Count of Monte Cristo. Romeo and Juliet. The Great Gatsby. Robinson Crusoe. Harry Potter.*

On and on it goes, until I sit surrounded by lives I could easily pretend to live for a few hours, to escape with, a sort of freedom. And there is a sense of curiosity about what I would discover, a feeling that has never been there before. It fills my emptiness with intrigue.

At the end of the pile, the last volume catches my attention. The size is flat and narrow, not a novel. The cover depicts a woman who looks to be asleep, golden hair curling around a wonderfully serene face. *The Sleeping Beauty.*

I open the first page and realize it is an art book of sorts, a children's picture book. My mother used to read them to me, but I cannot recall the tales. All I know is the story will be told through wonderful images, paintings like the ones I used to decorate my room. In this foreign space, the familiarity comforts me. So I lean back against the wall, cradling this volume against my thighs.

In the first spread, I meet a king and queen. Elegant and beautiful, they seem peaceful in a way no queen I have ever known has. In the woman's arms, a tiny baby girl, adorable and smiling, eyes green like mine.

I flip the page, continuing as a series of gifts are presented to the little girl. Beauty. Musicality. Grace. All things I have never had a need for, all gifts that seem frivolous to me, until the last—death. But I turn the page, and the baby girl is saved, the curse is softened to sleep, a long sleep.

Another turn and years have passed, the baby has become a beautiful woman. Golden curls flow down to her back, an elegant dress frames her body, and she is loved by everyone. It is her birthday and she is alone for the first time in her life, free to do as she pleases, so she wanders the halls, exploring. An old woman spinning thread is all she finds, but it is enough, and she pricks her finger, falling into a deep sleep. The entire town follows her, one by one, until the kingdom itself vanishes into a dream.

The story turns to a prince, hunting, who happens upon this forgotten castle, frozen in time, cold. He is the only one awake, the only one who feels, and he breathes life into the empty hallways of the palace. Until he sees the princess, sleeping peacefully, and he touches his palm to her face.

I flip the page, but it is blank.

The story is over, incomplete. Ridges rest unevenly along the bind. The ending has been torn out, ripped free, and all I can wonder is why.

For the first time, I want to see how it ends. I want to know.

I move backward to the previous page, running my fingers along the prince's face as Asher's features fill my mind.

He's left a message for me, but I don't know what it is. I don't understand. I flip the page again, letting my fingers scratch against torn paper.

Does the prince save her?

Does the woman wake?

Does the town?

Somehow, it seems important. The answer is on the tip of my tongue. I want my blind eyes to see.

A small flame flickers in my chest, burning hot, willing Asher to show me.

Nine

I am too used to telling time by the rise and fall of the sun. Down here, surrounded by artificial light and concrete windows, my senses are confused. Sleep comes at seemingly random times, a quick yawn and my lids flutter closed. Only short knocks and dinner plates, or guided trips to the toilet down the hall, interrupt me. No one speaks to me. Asher has not come to see me again.

Which is why I jolt in surprise when a knock sounds, soft and gentle, almost as though I imagined it. I put my book aside, leaving the lost boys to their own devices for a little while, and slide from the bed.

Hesitantly, the door rolls open, slow enough that it seems pushed by a ghost. Then a blond head pokes through, eyes closed.

"Can I come in?" Asher asks, uncertainty etched in his face, as though he is almost afraid of something.

"Sure." I shrug.

His grin returns and the door swings wide, slamming against the stone with a smack. Hands crossing over his chest, Asher leans back against the wall, completely calm, eyes surveying the room and landing on the neat stack of books in the corner.

"Find anything you like?"

Ignoring his question, I walk over and pull the book of pictures from the pile. I've been ruminating for however long I've been stuck here, wondering why the pages were torn, what message he was trying to send me, if any at all.

"Did you do this?" I ask, flipping to the end, holding the empty binding out before me.

"Me?" His eyes go wide—too wide.

"I want to know how it ends."

"So you liked it then?" He casts a sidelong glance in my direction, a wicked smile on his lips.

"Does that matter?" I keep my tone calm, refusing to give in to his game.

"It matters," he says quietly, more to himself than to me, before snatching the book from my hands to flip through the pages. At one point he stops, running his fingers over the paper, stuck on an image I can't see, stuck on something he seems to be hiding.

Now I am certain it was a test, a way to gauge my reaction, but for what purpose I do not understand. Still, I want to know, I feel as though that art now belongs to me—the prince gave it up.

"So?" I ask, bending my fingers, holding them back so I do not snatch the volume free from his hands.

Asher looks up, an almost haunted look flashes over his features, quickly covered by the jovial face I recognize. He closes the book and hands it back to me, but for the first time his actions feel empty. "It ends happily," he says, voice resigned almost. "The prince wakes the princess, the evil fairy is destroyed, and the kingdom returns to its former glory."

"How does he wake her?" I sense that something has been left out of his tale.

A spark lights his eye. I did not realize I missed it until it reappeared, comforting me, bringing fire back to his otherwise cool face. "I'll save that lesson for another day."

Again, I feel left out of a joke, or the butt of one. But before I can reply, a cough in the doorway grabs my attention.

A girl waits there, around my age, though she seems more alive somehow. Her dark cheeks are flushed rosy, her brown eyes are wide and excited, her body seems to give off an energy that mine has never had.

"Hi," she squeaks, as though she just cannot contain herself.

"Jade, this is Maddy. Maddy, Jade."

Asher stands back as the girl rushes forward, presenting her hand. My face tightens, and I fight the urge to step back, instead lifting my hand slowly into hers. As soon as our fingers touch, her grip clamps, swishing my hand up and down until my arm feels like rubber, boneless.

Finally, she releases and my arm falls limp to my side. Her gaze falls to Asher, lip partially bit, but he presents her with an encouraging nod.

I remain silent.

"Welcome to our home," she exclaims, voice bouncing against the walls of my tiny room. I'm made dizzy by her. "I'm sorry I'm so excited, but I've just never met one of you before. Someone from Kardenia, I mean. Oh, I mean, I guess we have Asher, but he doesn't really count. He's not, you know, under the queen's thrall."

Maddy raises her hands next to her face and her eyes go wide, wiggling her fingers as though casting a spell.

My jaw slackens and my gaze slips to the side, looking pointedly at Asher, silently pleading with him to do something. A shrug is my response. A shrug and a smile—a smile I suddenly want to slap from his face.

"Oh it's okay," she continues, "you don't have to say anything. I mean, you're really overwhelmed, right? And well, we've all been told that people under the thrall tend to… How should I put this nicely? Act like total jerks. But it's not your fault, so don't worry, I won't hold it against you. I mean, you could, like say something, but…"

She trails off into silence, watching me expectantly, wriggling her hands. I lick my lips, unused to so much frenzied conversation. Life in Kardenia is slow, calm. There are no surprises, no outbursts, everyone moves at almost the same pace.

"Nice to meet you," I mutter, but that is all she needs and a bright smile infiltrates her features, stretching wide, and she takes my elbow into her hand.

"Asher asked me to take you to the bathing area of the compound, no boys allowed sort of thing, so just follow me. It's like sort of a maze down here if you don't know where to go, but you don't look like you'll have any trouble keeping up. I hear you're part of the queen's guard, I wish I knew how to fight. I mean, don't get me wrong, I, I will..." She pauses, looking to Asher for assistance.

"You're not going to punch her, are you?" He asks, but the conversation has totally lost me at this light speed. "Jade?"

"Huh?" I murmur, turning to face him, until the words all register. "Oh no, I won't try to run away if that's what you're asking. Not yet, anyway." I add the last bit just for shock value. Success. Maddy is silenced for a moment, and my mind has time to catch up.

"She's kidding," Asher asserts, but the force of his inspection suggests otherwise. I do what I do best, remain stoic and still, unaffected.

A nervous laugh escapes the girl's lips. A little thrill vibrates up my throat, a little buzz lights my heart—the warmth is unnatural, but I wonder if this is what joy feels like.

"Anyway," she says, pulling me toward the door, continuing as if nothing happened, "let's go. Later, Asher," she calls over her shoulder.

My head fights to spin around, to get one more glance at the prince before we leave, but I remain as I am, facing forward.

Maddy continues to babble as we walk arm in arm toward the baths. I learn that the compound is one of many, that other rebel networks still stand all over the world working to bring down the magic. So far, none have been successful. Electricity is mostly down everywhere, since the old grid has been destroyed by the new layout of the land, but salvaged solar panels and windmills still create usable energy for humans.

I also hear of their lives, stuck underground, basking in the few modern conveniences they were able to preserve, trying to continue on as normal as possible. There are still schools and teachers, still a variety of jobs for people to pursue, still goals like life and love and family that people yearn for.

Though she bounces from topic to topic, I try to keep my mind focused on her words, paying close attention so I can follow her meandering thoughts. With my concentration elsewhere, the surroundings blur. As far as I'm concerned, we walk in circles through this maze, one I do not wish to unveil. My instincts fight to map the path, to lock it in my mind, but I must not give myself an exit, a way to escape. Better that I am trapped here following the queen's orders. I will not give myself a way out of the choice I've made.

I'm also distracted by Maddy herself. By the kindness in her tone, the way our arms intertwine as though we're connected, by the openness with which she speaks. Affection has never been a strong part of my life, at least since the earthquake. I've forgotten what companionship might feel like, but listening to her speak, a memory resurges just out of reach.

"Here we are."

The two of us stop just before a door, which Maddy pulls open before guiding me inside. Curtains line the walls. Water rushes out of sight. Steam seeps up through slits in the ceiling. The light here is yellow, bright, and I realize we are close to the surface. Above my head are grates, barring any exit, but still, I can just make out the sun. My breath comes easier. After so many years on the wall, so many years of candles and firelight, I am relieved to escape the dim blue lights of the rebel base.

"Welcome to the girl's shower room." Maddy keeps walking in deeper and I follow. "There's only one because it took forever for people to figure out the plumbing, cause we needed to loop an internal system without using any drinkable water up. But, I mean, it works and we still get to shower once a week, so it's okay. Some of the adults remember the good old days, back before the earthquake, but once you get used to it, it feels pretty normal. And you've been to the toilets, I mean, I hope you have. We have a few of those, but that plumbing system is totally different and way closer to your part of the compound."

"Once a week?" The question slips out before I can stop it. Her tone sounded dismissive, but once a week sounds wonderful. I am used to cold baths and infrequent ones at that.

"Ugh, I know, but it's not that bad."

I nod, hiding the grin from my face, itching to test the showers. Water falls from spouts in the wall, if I remember correctly. I've seen them during scavenging trips, in every apartment, but we never tried to make them work.

"Go ahead, I'll be back in a little while. We're only supposed to use the showers for like ten minutes, but I won't tell."

As though we are conspiring to hide a great secret, she waves goodbye, but the silence is welcome, and I pause for a minute, staring at the wall of curtains before me. One is likely no better than the other, so I just select at random, pulling a blue panel to the side before stepping in.

Like I suspected, a shiny nozzle is attached to the ceiling and below it a handle. On the opposite wall there is a hook waiting empty, and another holding soaps of different varieties.

My clothes are quickly abandoned and left on the floor. Dirty from the days of travel on the road. Smelly from my own sweat. I am happy to let the uniform fall away. Stains discolor my skin, so, almost urgently, I turn the knob.

Water slaps my face and I step back, caught off guard by the cold as a yelp escapes my lips. The water numbs like shards of ice, prickling my skin, but in the small space, there is nowhere to escape, so I wait as the onslaught continues. This water is no different from what we use at home, only it sprays at me and does not sit idle in a tub.

Then suddenly, it warms. Grows hotter still until steam filters up before my eyes. I sigh, standing below the steady stream as my muscles relax, running my hands through the knots in my hair, bringing my face as close to the spout as I possibly can.

This is amazing.

A smile presses into my lips and I laugh, heart bubbling like it did with the light switch, somehow buoyant.

I grab the soap, rubbing my hands over my skin until I am coated in white bubbles. The smell of flowers infiltrates my nose, sweet, lemony too. And then, under the water, the suds simply fall away, leaving behind a cleanliness I have never known. We had soap back home, but it never left the skin, and I would emerge from my tub feeling oily, shaking with shivers, dreading the next time I would return.

But this I never want to leave.

"Jade?" Maddy calls over the noise of the water. I groan, wishing to be invisible, to blend with the water. "I have clothes for you, if you want them, I mean."

My own clothes are a heap on the ground, white from soap, dripping with water, too dark in this already dark place. I nudge them away with my foot, only pausing to remove my black heart pin. That, I've earned. That, I will not abandon. It's a good reminder that this life is only a dream, and my real destiny waits back home, with the commander and the queen.

Relishing my last few moments of peace, I sigh and turn the water off. The instant the stream disappears, my arms feel cold. The chill returns and the heat melts away, drifting up to the sky along with the steam.

A hand pushes through the curtain. "Here!"

Jeans and a green shirt are dangling from her fingers, so I snatch them, hastily getting dressed.

"That was great," I tell her as I pull the curtain aside. Instantly, her expression warms, seemingly happy that I'm more relaxed. And I realize that this entire time, all of her rambling was an attempt to make me feel more comfortable, less alone, less like a prisoner.

Friends are not something I've ever needed. But an ache in my gut urges me to try, urges me to want.

"That's the first time since the earthquake that I've showered." The words come slowly through my lips. I force them out.

"Really?" Her eyes go wide and she leans in, grabbing my arm. "I can't believe that. I mean, none of us really know what goes on inside Kardenia, but I never thought...wow."

"Yeah," I nod. No more conversation fills my mind. I have no more brilliant words to say.

I'm totally and utterly blank. Useless.

"Do you want this?" Maddy asks, presenting me with a hairbrush, which I gladly accept, if just for something to do aside from stand there awkwardly mute. "So what's it like? Kardenia, I mean."

"Like?" I hesitate, thinking. "Any life I guess. People work and sleep and eat. Nothing unusual except for people like me, who remember how it used to be, but we've adjusted."

"Yeah, but, how do you like live without any electricity, at all. I mean, even here things seem tough sometimes, but at least we have showers and refrigerators and things. You're like, medieval."

"I guess," I say, trying to keep the laughter from my voice. But it's a nice feeling, sort of, to connect with someone, to talk.

Maddy looks around, as though afraid someone might overhear us. Leaning in, she brings her lips close to my ear, about to ask something I sense is not allowed. "And aren't you all, like…" Pause. I don't move, worried she might stop, wondering what could be so secretive. "Well, I don't mean this to be rude, but like zombies?"

"Huh?" I turn to meet her eyes at the use of such an unfamiliar word. A pit clumps to life in my throat. I retreat, pull back.

Stupid.

I was so stupid to think...

At my silence, Maddy continues in a hushed voice. "You know, zombies, the living dead? Hasn't the queen like tapped out all of your emotions? We heard you can't really feel, well, anything."

My eyes turn sharp, squint, and I grip the brush harder as the chill returns to my limbs. The shower was only a temporary fix, a temporary warm. The ice is back in my chest, strong and full of shards.

I am less than human to these people.

But Maddy is right.

I am like the dead. And it was futile to think for even a second that I might come alive again.

"It's true," I say, voice like a knife, "we don't feel anything."

At least, we're not supposed to. The queen controls us, and I cannot forget that. I am never out of her sight. I am never free. Even here, underground, surrounded by a different sort of magic, I cannot escape her hold. Cannot escape the stain she left on me, the taint.

As I think it, her fingers, invisible in my chest, clutch my heart. They squeeze harder, as if sensing my doubts, draining it, emptying everything away until I am left once more with nothingness.

My soul is not my own.

No shower, friend, or prince is ever going to change that. And the quicker I remember, the better off I'll be.

I'm here for one thing and one thing only.

My freedom.

Ten

Maddy's words stick with me. I cannot shake them. I've spent the past day dissecting them, wondering if that is what all the rebels believe, wondering if I believe it too. Am I human? Am I something else? A puppet that the queen controls with strings. A zombie. A brainless, emotionless weapon. Can something like that ever be free?

Since leaving the showers, I have tried to firm my resolve. But my heart beats uncomfortably in my chest, and my palms grow moist. I couldn't sleep. Something foreign plagues my system, flurrying my insides, knotting and twisting them until I am consumed.

Betrayal.

It sounds so simple.

But for some reason, though I try to focus on my freedom, on what I stand to gain, my chest only feels pain at the idea of continuing my lies. Do I want to be the monster Maddy described, emotionless, thoughtless? No matter what

I do, every path seems to lead to that road, to the queen.

I don't think I have a choice.

A knock sounds at my door, soft, gentle. I don't move from my bed, suddenly alert, chest tight as I wait.

Asher's head pokes through first, hesitant, but when he sees me watching, fully clothed and perfectly awake, his casual attitude returns.

"Jade," he exclaims, slamming the door shut behind him, making sure I have no way out. Clearly, he doesn't trust me yet.

Good.

I don't. He shouldn't either.

"Asher," I say, surprising myself with the spring in my voice. There's a subtle chime in the tone, almost cheerful. I frown. What is happening to me?

"How were the showers?" He slips farther into the room, and I notice he's holding a few boxes in his arms, colorful ones.

"Good." I shrug, trying to stay calm. My heart seems to have a mind of its own and has decided to begin beating wildly in my chest, uncomfortably. I squirm, deciding to stand. Perhaps movement will help.

"Well, you look better."

I stop, turning to stare at him. "What does that mean?"

Asher's mouth drops open and his cheeks flush slightly pink. "Oh, um, nothing..." He looks around, then his eyes pop wide, and he shoves his arms out, presenting the boxes like a gift. "Board game?"

"Sure…" I drag out the word, not quite sure if I want to let him off the hook. Judging by his reaction, I know exactly what his comment meant.

Asher gets the message and quickly sits, spreading the boxes across the ground so I can see all the names and pictures. I join him on the floor, crossing my legs, unsure of what to do next. I'm used to solitude, to the wall, to wandering the city on my own. Idle time spent in the company of others is completely foreign to me.

"We have Monopoly, Scrabble, Connect Four, and Battleship. Your choice."

I study the lids. One has spelling tiles, one has lots of fake money, one just has black and red dots, and the other has an explosion.

Definitely the explosion.

"Battleship?"

Asher smirks. "I had a feeling you'd choose that one."

He pushes the other boxes aside and opens the game up, handing me a folding case with all sorts of pins and little plastic boats. I accept them, but my mind is utterly blank, completely confused as to what I do next. I'm used to real war games, the shooting yard, fencing drills, archery.

I glance at Asher for a clue, but he is bent over, biting his lip as he stares intently at his little box. I'm not even sure if I have mine the right way.

"Um?" I ask. He looks up, startled. "What am I supposed to do?"

"You've never played?" He looks shocked, but I'm not sure why.

"No."

He shuts his case, locking the ships inside. "Come on, we'll play one you already know."

I take a deep breath as a warm tingle travels up my chest, making me feel strange, out of place. "I don't know any of them."

"Oh, sorry." He leans back, frowning. "I just assumed you guys had games too, since you're right outside that big city. I mean, we didn't have them in Kardenia before I left, I just thought people might have found them."

"They did." I shrug, glancing at the games again. Some of them look familiar. I might have seen other Black Hearts playing or maybe some kids on the street.

Asher furrows his brows, confused. "So why didn't you play?"

His question is innocent enough, but in that moment, I realize something. Asher and I know absolutely nothing about each other. To me, he is just a prince. To him, I am just a Black Heart. Our pasts, our histories, all of that is blank. And that's how I've always known everyone. The commander is not my father, he is my leader, and I never cared to look deeper. The queen is just that, my queen. I don't need to understand who she is. Members of the guard are my coworkers. The butcher is the butcher. The seamstress is the seamstress. And so on, for almost everyone I've ever met.

But meeting the genuine curiosity in Asher's eyes, I want to introduce myself. Not the hard girl on the wall. The other girl, the one who came alive in the solace of my bedroom or during explorations of the city. The person no one but me has ever met. Maybe then I won't seem so much like a monster.

"I didn't have anyone to play with," I say, voice lower than normal, softer. "I grew up with the commander of the Black Hearts, no brothers or sisters or anything."

"No friends?" he asks.

I keep my gaze locked on the floor. "Not really. I spent most of my time training with him or by myself. The boys my age didn't really enjoy sparring with me. And well, the girls were more interested in clothes and things, so I stayed away. Once I was old enough to explore the city, I spent a lot of my time there, reading." I look up, finally meeting his gaze. "Just like you found me."

Asher leans forward, putting his hand over mine. It's warm, just like his eyes, filled with a light I've never seen before, soft and glowing. "Believe it or not, I understand exactly what you mean. Before I ran away, my life was one of solitude too. No family who cared. No friends either."

"Really?" I ask, biting my tongue before I reveal that he's the prince. I would have thought a life in the palace was filled with people, servants in the least. Though, as my mind wanders back to my interaction with the queen, walking those dark and empty halls, it's not so difficult to imagine. The bigger the home, the easier it is to be ignored. "Is that why you left?"

Asher leans back, pulling his hand away. "Sort of."

I want to know more. How he freed himself. How he escaped. Why he left when the entire kingdom was his to inherit. But I hold the questions in, sitting back. I'm not ready to tell him that I know who he is, not ready to give away that small upper hand, not ready to get so personal.

"Did you find what you were looking for here?" I ask instead, settling on an easier question.

"I did." He nods, genuine, honest. "I'll always be an outsider of sorts, I guess, because I'm from the magic world. But I found something here I never would have found back home."

"What?"

Asher smirks, shaking his head. "I can't tell you."

"Why not?" I fight the urge to cross my arms.

"It's just something you need to discover on your own. I'll tell you soon."

I lean forward, narrowing my eyes. "When?"

"When you're ready."

For what? I want to ask, but I don't. I keep it inside. Because I hear something in those words that frightens me, a sort of finality or inevitability. There is no doubt in Asher's mind that I will be ready at some point. He believes in me, which means he is beginning to trust me…maybe, just a little. But even that small amount is too much.

I'm unintentionally doing everything the queen asked. The more human I try to be, the more of a monster I seem to become.

But Asher is unaware of the turmoil thrumming through my veins as he pulls the case back out, turning it so I can see the plastic boats he attached to the board and the pile of pegs he's left untouched in a little side compartment.

"Okay, the first rule of Battleship is there is no Battleship."

"Huh?" I ask.

Asher rolls his eyes, shaking his head with a mysterious smile. "Never mind."

Eleven

Every day of the next week, Asher arrives at my door with a new game to teach me. The hours are filled with new rules to explain and new cheats to attempt. But they're also filled with something else, something new that I never expected.

Laughter.

Conversation.

I'm beginning to understand why the other guards on the wall passed the time playing cards and drinking beer, rather than standing alone in the dark like I did. The companionship is almost fun. The more I talk about my childhood, the easier it becomes and the more I reveal. Though Asher does not discuss his time with the queen, he tells me about life in the rebel camp. How it felt to grow up an outsider, how they eventually welcomed him into the fold.

I've discovered I'm a sore loser, as Asher labels it. But I call him a sore winner. More than once, I've had to stop myself from slapping the smirk off his lips. But the look on his face when I beat him at a game he's been playing his entire life is victory enough for me.

Though we talk a lot, there is still a divide—a line that seems to stretch between us. We do not pass beyond polite conversation. I do not make demands of him. We get close, but not close enough that he will trust me. Yet, against my better judgment, I'm curious about what might wait beyond that barrier. Will his smile grow deeper? Will his touch become more carefree? Will his words turn more open?

Will mine?

The doorknob turns, creaking, grabbing my attention.

Asher is back. I wait, heart in my throat. The sight of him has begun to put me off balance, to steal my thoughts, to make my mind jumbled. I'm not sure what it means, but I know that I've grown to like the loss of control, the small skip of excitement.

"Morning," he says.

I don't respond, my voice feels trapped, so instead, I offer up a smile.

"Okay, I brought something I think you'll really like. It's got more rules than normal, but it's very strategic so I think you'll really get into it."

Asher pauses when he sees my face.

I bite my lip, unsure if I should ask what I had been planning to ask.

But I miss the outdoors.

My eyes have adjusted to the dim blue lights of the rebel base, but my soul has not. I yearn for the trees, for the fresh air. My skin wishes to feel the kiss of the sun again. My muscles ache to stretch and to run. My body is not used to so much idleness, so much laziness. I'm made for action.

So I had decided that today I would gather enough courage to see if Asher will take me above ground. But watching him now, I'm not so sure.

"What?" His voice is wry, as though he can tell just by looking at me that there is something on my mind.

I breathe deeply, and then expel the words very quickly, all at once. "I was wondering if maybe you might take me outside."

He laughs and shakes his head. "Nope. Not happening."

"Why?" I ask. His reaction has caused my heart to race a little faster. He didn't even pause, didn't even think it over or consider it.

"Just because." He shrugs it off, opening the new game he's brought. But I step forward, confronting him, feeling impulsive.

"I'm serious, I really want to be outdoors for a little while."

He stops, lips wobbling while he tries to determine what to say. "Look, I'm sorry. I would take you outside, really, I would. But there are rules about that sort of thing at the base, so I can't."

"Rules for everyone, or just for me?" I peer at him, knowing he's hiding something.

"Well, if we had other prisoners, those would be the rules for them too..." Asher trails off, smiling meekly.

I step back as if hit. Though I've been acutely aware of my situation, I never realized that was how everyone here saw me, just as a prisoner. I didn't think that was how Asher saw me, not really. My insides harden as my chest cramps painfully.

"Jade," he says and reaches for my arm, but I back away.

"Why am I here?" I ask, abrupt and cold.

Asher flinches, blinking back in shock. "What do you mean?" He stammers.

"Why did you take me hostage? It can't be just to sit around and play board games all day. I'm surprised that's not against the rules too."

"Maybe I just thought you were cute." He shrugs, smiles, trying to make me forget with his jokes. But the blood in my arms has started to warm, it heats to an uncomfortable level. A drum pounds in my ears, growing faster, louder, blocking out every other sound.

It scares me. It intrigues me.

I don't want to back down, not when my gut is urging me to demand, to fight.

"Asher," I say, pressing for the truth. "Why am I here? Why did you bring me with you? Why me?"

My voice rises to a shout as my blood boils, stings, races through my veins zapping my body acutely to life. My vision turns scarlet as my energy builds.

I like the feeling.

I don't try to suppress it.

Asher cocks his head to the side, watching me, curious. A grin pulls at his cheeks as a spark ignites behind his indigo eyes—a challenge.

"I'm not going to tell you," he goads.

"Why?" My fists clench at my waist.

Suddenly, the gray walls of this room seem small, more confining than I ever realized. I miss the breeze on my cheeks, the fresh smell of grass, the vastness of the sky. The outdoors call to me, and I am done with this artificial world, this concrete prison. Asher really must think me idiotic if he thought that pretty curtains could hide the truth of what this room is. A cell.

I am hardly thinking anymore. The heart in my chest pounds hard against my ribs, as though it will jump free of my body. The thunder drowns out my ears as the heat under my skin begins to rise.

I no longer have reason.

I realize what I do have, what surges through my body as I watch Asher mock me. Fury. Anger.

Without warning, I scream in frustration and charge, swinging a fist at Asher's face, feeling a little thrill as his mouth drops open in shock. My muscles shout with glee to finally be used, to stretch and pull once more.

Asher catches my hand in his, so I punch with my left hand. He catches that one too and we are stuck, his back against the wall as I press into his frame.

I cannot move my arms, but I still have legs, so I shift my knee to deliver a hard blow, but Asher anticipates the move and pushes me backward. I stumble over my feet, feeling blinded by the rage burning my insides. My brain cannot concentrate on the fight and it makes me weak. That in turn only makes my blood boil more.

I charge.

He pushes me aside again, but I clutch his fingers, dragging his arms to the floor with me, and Asher's body follows. We tumble, arms and legs fold together, fight against each other.

Our arms lock, neither giving in. My hands grip his bicep, and his muscles harden as he grips mine. But I roll, gaining the upper hand and the higher position, pinning him as my legs tighten on his, constraining them so he cannot move.

Below me, his body rumbles, starts to shake.

My gaze travels slowly up to his face, knowing what I will find, and I am right. Silent laughter wracks his frame. I want to shake him, to hit him, but I can't move for fear of giving him the upper hand.

"What?" I snap. My mouth is the only part of me that is free to fight back. I breathe heavily. But so does he.

"You're angry." He smirks. "Really, really angry. It's fantastic."

"No, I'm not," I growl.

"Yes, you are. Trust me. I recognize real fury when I see it."

Our faces are close together, I suddenly realize. His lips are just a few inches below mine, flushed pink like his cheeks. His eyes consume my gaze, pull it in, drag me closer.

The heat in my veins shifts, just slightly, into something I do not recognize. An emotion I cannot place.

Panic fills me.

I must escape.

The single thought consumes my mind. I am not ready for whatever is happening, for this new sensation sending shivers down my spine, for the promise in his gaze.

Asher shifts below me. His grip slackens and his hands move slowly up my arms, over my shoulders, toward my neck. Gentle. Smooth.

I can't breathe.

"I'm not," I gasp and roll free of him, standing quickly, walking to the far corner of the room, putting as much distance between us as possible. I gulp down air, shove it into my chest, calm my racing pulse. I pray for the freeze to return, for my limbs to grow cold, to grow familiar.

This madness is not me.

I am steady. I am a rock. I am not the storm that rages and spits fire into the sky.

"What is happening to me?" I whisper.

But a hand lands softly on my shoulder, and I remember that I'm not alone, that my question had waiting ears. I turn, eyes drifting over my shoulder.

"It's okay, Jade," Asher soothes.

"It's not." I shake my head, step back, out of his almost embrace.

"You're allowed to feel, people are supposed to feel," he urges, voice heavy and full of passion. I try to believe him, I want to, but the freeze is so much easier. I am used to winter. I am okay with it.

I step back until I touch the wall, until I am cornered with nowhere else to go.

"You're ready for the truth, and the truth is I felt like you do once," Asher says, following me to the wall, trapping me, enveloping me in the kindness in his voice. His hand comes to my face, cupping my cheek as his thumb runs gently over my skin.

I don't know what to say. Speech has left me. But there are unspoken words surging up my throat, ones I know I should not say, a confession I know I cannot voice. My body yearns to tell him the truth, to tell him why I am here. But I can't, not now, not when he's looking at me like that. Instead, I tell him another truth. One I've owed him.

"I know you're the queen's son," I murmur, but my voice is loud enough to cross the small space between our bodies.

He stills for a moment, sighs while his shoulders fall just slightly. "I guessed as much. But that only means you know that I'm telling the truth. Jade, I lived in old Kardenia for the first few years of my life, surrounded by a populace that cannot feel, cursed with a mother who stole everyone else's emotions yet turned none of them onto her only child. And I know now, after living here for so long, that that is not how life is supposed to be."

He shakes his head, lets it fall. I remain silent.

"People are supposed to laugh and love. A mother should cry when she births her first child, she shouldn't sit there silently, not bothering to ask to hold her baby. When someone dies, it should be a sad thing. It should tear your chest in two. Life is full of highs and lows, of passion and grief. It shouldn't trot forward at a steady pace of nothingness. But my mother is a selfish woman, so she uses her magic to fuel her own heart, to experience everyone else's love and everyone else's sorrow, to fill the void in her chest."

"How did you escape?" I ask. Freedom is all I want—it's everything. How did he grasp it? How can I?

"On the day our worlds merged, even though I was just a boy, I felt hope for the first time. Armies came and I saw people filled with passion, filled with fear and love and drive, and I knew there was another way. So I ran, looking for these people who dared fight the queen. Wanting more than anything to join them."

"But how?" I ask. "How did you escape her thrall?"

Asher looks away, to the floor, and I realize I have lost him. He is hiding something. A secret he will not tell me. A sure sign that he does not trust me.

But that is for the better.

I shrink free of his embrace and he lets me go. The queen gave me an impossible task. Trust cannot be given to the heartless.

But somehow, I don't feel so heartless anymore. Because I was furious. My blood burned. The rage in my chest now evaporates, like a ghost, disappearing rapidly as my body returns to its normal blankness. But it was there.

"I think maybe I was angry," I confess, "but it's gone now."

Asher's face lights up, excited, and I recognize that this is the hope he was talking about. "It's working then."

"What?"

"You wanted to know why I took you, why I captured you? Because of what you just said. I needed to know if it is possible for an adult to be released from the spell, to be freed from the queen, to learn to feel. You've crossed over beyond her reach, and it looks like maybe, the effects are starting to wear off."

"You mean?" I trail off into silence, afraid to say it out loud.

Maybe I am human after all.

Maybe I can be free.

But I don't need to speak the words, the hope, because I can see that Asher knows them already. That he felt them too, years ago in his own childhood. And I can tell that he believes them.

I break contact first.

I want to believe, I truly do, but part of me cannot. I dread that the queen is playing a trick on me, is dangling everything I've ever dreamed of before my eyes, waiting until the perfect time to snatch it all away.

Still, I promise myself that I'll try.

"Jade?" Asher questions. I don't turn around. I'm not sure if I can face the steadfast faith in his eyes.

"Yes?"

"Can you promise me something?"

I nod, still not spinning, not daring to even speak. We've just reached the end. The line rests before us, and I know Asher is going to cross it, is going to drag me with him. After his words, nothing will be the same.

"No one here knows I'm the prince. They believe I was a servant in the queen's castle and that's why I know so much. If they knew who I really was, they would never look at me the same way. They would always doubt me. Please, I'm trusting you to be silent."

There is that word.

Trust.

It shoves into my back, pushes inside of me, fills me up.

I don't want to look at him, but I do. The stars in his eyes sparkle. His face holds no ounce of mockery, no smile, no frown, just an openness that welcomes me, that urges me to believe him.

I want to tell him I do not deserve his trust. That I did not earn it. That I cannot have it.

I want to tell him that the queen sent me for this exact moment, because she knew his gentle soul ached for someone who understood him, who he could save like he did himself.

I want to tell him I'm a liar. That in the end I will betray him. That I can only bring him pain.

All these things surge to my lips, but I silence them. Because there is a new flame sparking to life in my chest, a fire I do not want to put out, a burn slowly melting the ice encasing my insides. I don't know what it is, but I know that if I tell Asher the truth, the fire will die and I will never find it again.

"I promise."

We have crossed over to the other side, to a world entirely new to me, one that scares yet also excites me. And I know we can never go back.

Asher leaves without another word.

I collapse onto my bed, drained.

More than anything, I want to believe that I chose this, that I am worthy of the trust I was just bestowed, that I will live up to the hope in Asher's eyes.

That I can be human.

But a darkness lingers at the back of my mind, whispering in a musical voice that everything is falling perfectly into place.

Twelve

"Jade?"

A voice I do not quite recognize interrupts my solace. I am lying still on my bed, staring at the wall, utterly conflicted. Mental turmoil has exhausted my body, a sensation I am unused to, but it is not entirely unwelcome. Still, I come alive at the sound of that voice, wanting the distraction. So I turn, surprised to see Maddy at the door.

She is slumped against the frame, noticeably lacking the energetic bubble I assumed perpetually floated with her body. But her expression is muted, hesitant. Her voice was low, which is why I did not recognize it.

"Hey." I sit up, nodding that she is welcome to come in. But she remains by the door. I search for fear in her eyes, worried she thinks me contagious, that the curse can spread.

Maddy opens her mouth. Closes it. Shuffles her feet, anxious. Then four words slip through her lips. "Jade, I'm really sorry."

I inhale, breath swelling with my heart, which seems to expand in my chest. Looking up under hooded brows, her gaze meets mine, waiting. I realize she is not afraid of me, she is afraid of being rejected.

People do not apologize where I'm from. Years of being bullied by my peers, beat down by the boys, given no aid by the commander, and I have never once received remorseful words. I have learned not to expect them. I do not know how to accept them.

My natural instinct is to disconnect, to ignore.

I had already written Maddy off. She thought me a zombie, so I deemed her unworthy of my time. Done. Finished.

But watching her now, I am unsure. And that is enough to make me want to hear more.

"Sorry for what?" I question, trying to keep the steel from my voice.

Her expression brightens just slightly and she steps free from the wall, moving imperceptibly farther into the room.

"For what I said, I mean, calling you a zombie. It was stupid, and I didn't mean it the way it sounded, and I could tell that I hurt your feelings, which means that you totally have them, and that I was wrong, and..."

Maddy trails off, antsy as she shifts her weight from side to side. The energy in her body starts to build, unused to being suppressed for so long.

I'm not sure if Asher sent her to test me, to push on my newfound emotions, to see if she can ignite a different flare. But I don't care. This isn't about him, not completely. I promised myself that I would try to discard the monster, to act the human, to live up to the trust I've been bestowed.

This is my first trial.

Even though it is hard, I lick my lips, forcing unfamiliar words to my voice. "I forgive you."

The mood in the room shifts, zipping to life as a smile widens Maddy's cheeks and she jumps closer to me. My mood follows, soaring higher, feeling lighter.

"Thank you," she gushes, grasping my upper arm in her hand. "I was hoping you would say that. And just in case, you know, you forgave me, I had an idea planned. Just a suggestion, really, I mean you don't need to listen to me."

"No, please," I say, feeling caught in her whirlwind but not bothered by it. The opposite in fact. Her energy bubbles over, teaching my calm body how to feel alive.

"Okay, great." She tugs on my hand, bringing me to the floor where we both sit across from one another with legs folded. A stack of cards almost magically appears in her hands and she deftly shuffles, weaving the cards in an out with a grace I didn't think her frenetic body possessed. But her fingers are nimble, focused.

"Well, I was thinking," she says, not bothering to watch the cards and instead focusing her attention on me. "It's not so much that you can't connect with people, but more like you don't know how. I mean, Asher's told us about the way life was for him, how people didn't seem to care about each other. But that doesn't mean you can't, not really, more like you've just never been allowed to."

"Okay," I say slowly, squirming a little, not sure I like where this is going.

"Anyway, the best way to feel connected to someone is to talk with them and to open up, you know? At least, I think so. But you don't really seem like the sharing type." Maddy pauses, eyes going wide. "I mean, no offense."

I shrug. "I'm not."

A sigh rushes from her body as the excitement returns. "So basically, I thought we could play a game. All the girls used to play this when we were younger, you know, to try to get someone to confess to a secret crush or admit something embarrassing, you know."

I don't, but I remain silent. Growing up, other little girls were not my friends, not my companions. We did not play together. I've certainly never whispered secret confessions into their ears.

"But," Maddy continues, unaware of the way my thoughts have wandered, "we would play just to learn more about each other, to you know, get to know each other. Like friends."

A twinge heats my spine. Nerves. They tingle as they travel through my body, and I recognize my own fear surging to life.

"What game?" I ask, throat dry. After the fight with Asher, I'm not so sure if games are a great idea anymore.

"It's really simple," Maddy urges, cutting the deck and delivering half of the cards into my sweating palm. "Basically, we each flip a card over. Whoever has the higher card gets to ask a question, and the loser has to tell the truth. If it's just numbers, the questions have to be yes or no. But if you win with a face card, then the loser has to actually explain. And we can play for however long we want, I mean, it almost never lasts until the cards run out, cause someone used to get upset and run away."

Maddy laughs suddenly, leaning in closer, whispering to me. "We used to get so mad, as kids I mean. Because you would lose to a face card, and then there was always one girl who would make you confess which boy you wanted to kiss or, you know, some other nonsense and the loser would start crying. I think the adults wanted to ban it for a while."

As Maddy shakes her head at the memory, I try to envision such a scene, of girls hanging out together, plotting to unveil each other's secrets. Torturing each other in a way only those with feelings could really be tormented. My childhood, emotionless as it was, doesn't seem so bad.

But I watch Maddy, noting how her eyes crinkle and glitter with enjoyment, how they sparkle against her dark skin. None of my memories incur such a reaction, none since the earthquake anyway.

My hands itch to begin, and at the same time, we

both flip a card.

I win, my seven beating her three.

"Are you happy?" I ask. I'm not sure why, it is just the first thing that pops out.

"Yes," Maddy says without hesitation.

We flip. I win again—ten over eight. A smile spreads my lips as I get an odd pleasure at the sight.

"Do you believe in the resistance?"

"Yes." Again, not a drop of insecurity.

This time I present a queen, overruling her four. Luck, it seems, is finally on my side. "What do you do for the resistance?"

"Right now, I'm a little too young to really do much. I go to the surface to look for supplies. I scout sometimes. But I'm training to become a doctor, like a healer if you don't remember what that is."

"Why?" I ask, curious. All my life, I've been a fighter. I've never once thought about keeping another person alive.

But Maddy shakes her head, sly. "You have to win another card first."

We draw. I lose, but not to a face card.

"Do you remember your life, before the earthquake I mean?"

I pause. Parts of it used to filter into my mind, hazy, distorted. But the longer I remain with the rebels, the clearer my memories have become. My mother's face floats before my eyes, more exact than I've seen it before, and I sort of remember her—the way being around her made life better, the way it used to feel like home. "Yes."

I lose again. This time to a jack.

Maddy pauses, biting her lip, and I can tell she does not want to waste her opportunity to glimpse past my façade, to open me up. "Have you ever been in love?"

I know what she means. With a boy, with a man. In truth, I've never even kissed one. I've never wanted to. But that is not the only sort of love there is. "I think once a long time ago, I loved my mother and she loved me. That's probably not what you mean, but it's the only memory I have. Sometimes, when I think of her, I feel it still, a little spark that pulls me toward her."

I blink, recoiling and shutting my mouth. Those words have never passed my lips, have never been said out loud. But Maddy looks on encouragingly, and I force myself not to turn away, to continue on this path no matter how scary.

We flip again.

"Have you ever been in love?" I ask, turning her own question against her.

"Yes." A secret tugs her lips upward.

Urgent, I flip. I win again.

"With a boy?"

"Yes."

"Are you still in love?" I ask, cursing myself for the lack of face cards. I want a real explanation.

"Yes."

I sit back, rocked by a heaviness filling my lungs, forming into a clump in my throat. My eyes sting.

But I lose the next round, silencing me and I sigh, wondering what this tightness is, knowing my answer will not come soon.

"Have you ever met the queen?"

"Yes," I say but empty my mind. I do not want to think of that woman.

"What was your favorite part of life back in Kardenia?" Maddy asks, taking advantage of a face card win with a king.

"The wall," I say quickly, no speck of doubt in my mind. "Walking the wall always felt very peaceful, sort of like I was alone, stuck in between two different worlds. And beyond the wall, exploring the city, I liked that too. The buildings, the museums, the library. All of it just waiting for me."

Another question whirls in her mind, flashing behind her eyes, but she holds back, abiding by the rules.

"You can ask," I tell her, putting my cards to the side.

"What is New York like? Now, I mean, abandoned and everything. I've seen pictures from before and scenes from movies and things."

"Still majestic, in an odd sort of way. I'm told it used to smell, from all of the people who died during the earthquake, but it's been a long time since then. A lot of the guards still don't like it out there, but I do. There's something beautiful about the destruction. Not the broken parts, but when you find a place that is untouched, unchanged, like a moment trapped in time." I shrug, unsure of how to explain it.

But it's like the library—the windows are broken, the chandeliers have fallen to the ground, the walls are covered in grime. But, my breath still catches when I enter. Or when I happen across an apartment that hasn't been gazed upon in more than a decade. There are still clothes hanging in the closet, still dishes in the washer, still an unmade bed, and it feels like I've found something secret, as though the world itself is dreaming.

There is a different sort of magic that lingers in the old buildings, pockets of wonder I can't begin to explain.

But Maddy accepts my words, as lacking as they were, and her eyes blank just a little as she tries to imagine the scene. In turn, I wonder how odd it must be to live life underground when the whole world waits just a few feet overhead.

"Can I ask you something?"

My words startle her, but Maddy instantly nods her head, multiple times, and her face lights up. Her cards, I notice, have also been discarded. But that was the whole point after all.

Two questions linger in the back of my mind, but I choose the easier one. We have left talk of love behind, and my mind feels clearer, less constricted. I will ask her about it eventually, when I am ready, when the idea does not overwhelm me.

"Why do you want to be a doctor?"

"My father," she says quietly, barely a whisper. A gentle expression stretches across her face, smoothes it, relaxes it, until I almost do not recognize her. The pent up energy is submerged under whatever memory holds her captive. "My dad, he was an army doctor."

"Was?"

Maddy looks up, eyes downturned just slightly. "I mean, I guess he still could be, but I haven't seen him since the earthquake. He was part of the original teams that marched on Kardenia, you know, back in the early days before we really knew what we were fighting. I don't think any of them returned."

Then she meets my gaze, pleading.

And I understand.

I speed through my thoughts, faces flashing before my eyes, but none matches with hers. I shake my head slightly. Maddy blinks once, holding her eyes closed just a second too long, before opening and shrugging it off.

But I grab her hand, suddenly anxious to make her feel better, to turn the fake smile into a real one, to bring this energetic girl back to life.

"There are tons of people in Kardenia, and I know barely any of them. I don't even think I could name all the members of the guard, just the few I work with. Your dad could still be there."

Hope glimmers in her irises, a caramel streak brightening to life.

And in that instant, I know why I'm here. Why the rebels allowed Asher to take me hostage. Clarity stills my mind, slows it, pushing all the questions aside until there is just truth.

The rebels are all desperate to know if the queen's curse can be lifted. Not so they can defeat her. Not to win this war. Not for glory.

For love.

I never once wondered about the families all the trapped rebels left behind once they were pulled under the queen's thrall. But all the old earthlings who now live in Kardenia came from somewhere else. I left my mother. The others, it seems, left families too.

The difference between our two sides has never been clearer. While the rebels held on, hoped, fought to bring their families back together, we of Kardenia moved on, forgot, let go.

Suddenly my chest burns in pain, exploding down my stomach until I am ill. My eyes sting, they water. My hands tremble with my jaw, and I am heaving, gasping for air. The room is made of liquid and I am drowning, pulled under by the wave of conflicting emotions crashing through my helpless body.

"Jade?" Maddy asks as concern fills her eyes. Concern I bet she feels for her father. Concern I have never once bestowed upon my mother.

Where is she?

Is she alive?

Does she fight to find me?

Is she risking everything for a child who has abandoned her?

A hand rubs my arm as soothing words are whispered into my ear and an arm encircles my body.

I sob.

From hurt. From guilt. From confusion.

Maddy, with no explanation as to why my mood has so drastically shifted, comforts me.

And I am glad I'm not alone.

Thirteen

"Jade?"

It is Asher, but I do not move. I cannot move. My muscles reject my commands. They have lost all strength. It has flowed away in my tears, cries that are endless. I face the gray wall, eyes closed, still on the bed, curled into a ball.

When Maddy left, I dragged my lifeless body into this position, and it has not changed since then. Food has come, but it sits stale on the floor.

Now it seems Asher has been called in to break my mourning. But I do not want it to end—my mother deserved more from me, and now I will cry for her the way I should have done before. With a heart that has learned to feel.

"Jade, what's wrong?" His voice is heavy with worry.

The bed dips below me, giving me enough warning that I do not flinch as his palm just barely touches my shoulder, caressing it one time before dropping away.

But my hand reacts, and my fingers grasp his, holding them against my arm, relishing the small comfort they provide. I tug, and without words, he understands.

Gentle, as though timid, the bed dips further under his full weight. The warm hand I hold adjusts, wrapping around my body, pulling me closer to him in a firm hug. My back brushes against his stomach. His chin rests against the nook of my neck. Even our toes touch. His other arm swoops underneath me, until I am surrounded by Asher, warmed by him.

My heart slows to match his pace. My breath does too.

We sit like that, silent, as tears continue to fall from my eyes. He does not pressure me to speak, does not push and prod to understand, just accepts that I need help and offers it willingly.

My body is at peace. My mind eventually follows. It is a deeper sense of calm than I've ever been able to achieve in my solitude. Asher keeps me grounded, allowing me to float away, to drift without fear that I won't be able to return, to get lost in my own mind.

I wonder if that's what crossing the line was all about. Does trusting each other mean needing each other too? Because that's how I feel, like I don't know where I'd be if he wasn't here holding me. I turn in his arms so I can see the soft smile on his lips, the hazy glow in his eyes.

"My mother," I say, wanting those words to convey

so much but knowing how bare they sound. I want to make him understand, to show him a deeper truth inside me.

"What happened to her?" Asher whispers. His breath brushes my cheek, hot in the small space between our faces.

I shake my head as the muscles in my face constrict, tighten.

"Shh," Asher soothes, using his thumb to brush the tears from my wet cheeks.

"I..." My voice is scratchy. The words wobble from my lips, unsteady. Breathing deeply, I try again. "I don't know."

My last memory of my mother is hearing her screams. I had turned my back on her, running to the queen, believing her a princess from my storybooks come to save us in the aftermath of the earthquake. I ignored her plea to stop, to come back. I ripped free of her embrace, exchanging it for the touch of a woman who abused my naïve faith.

But that is not the worst part.

The worst part is that until now, I never stopped running, never once looked back and wondered what became of her.

"I don't know if she is alive or dead. I don't know if she still searches for me. And..." I pause, feeling small. "I never cared, Asher."

"You care now."

"Now it's too late."

Without warning, Asher sits up, yanking on my hand, forcing me to follow. His eyes have gone wide, energy sparks along his skin, blushing it to life.

"Come with me," he says.

I could tear my hand away and fall back to the bed, back to my solitude. But something in his voice, the steadfastness, the conviction, it urges me to give in. And I do, letting him pull me from the soft mattress as my muscles protest and my feet stumble to find their footing.

"My father died when I was only a few weeks old," he tells me as we continue down the halls. I am distracted by the warmth of his fingers, still holding onto my hand, not letting go but rather gripping tighter.

Asher keeps talking. "My mother poisoned him." I don't respond. The queen mentioned the story, dismissively, without an ounce of pain or concern. "I don't even remember him—not his face, or his voice, or anything. And I used to hate myself for that. I thought it made me just as cold as my mother. But as I grew up, I realized none of that was my fault. Just like none of what happened to you is your fault."

He squeezes my hand, and though we keep walking, I turn my eyes from the hall only to see that Asher is already watching me. What does he see?

As I gaze at him now, I see the sad little boy who grew up in a lonely household. No father. Just a mother who didn't care, who showed him no love, and stole away the love any other person might have given him. My mother was taken from me, but at least in my memories, I remember her warm smile and the words that effortlessly rolled from her lips, whispering that I meant everything.

I break contact, looking ahead, wanting to cry for him but forcing my will to be strong. How did a boy who grew up like that learn to show so much compassion?

"And I thought it was too late too. I knew he was dead. I understood that he was never coming back. But there were other ways I could honor him, just like there are other ways you can honor your mother."

"How?" I ask. Asher means well, but he ran away from the queen given the chance, and I let myself remain trapped. I never tried to escape, never tried to remember. Yet there is such faith in his voice, I cannot help but think he might be right. Maybe I can make amends.

"By helping other people find the loved ones they search for."

We turn a corner and I gasp.

A cavernous room rests before us, a large square space signifying a dead end. But that is not what enthralls me. It is what surrounds me. Everywhere I look, there are faces. Hundreds, maybe even a thousand, stare back at me. I drop Asher's hand, compelled, reeled in by the sight.

Photographs.

I have seen them before, in broken frames or tattered old books, glimpses of the past in the decaying city I've raided for years. But I've never had such a visceral reaction. It's as though these people jump out from the walls, hands grabbing for me, tugging me closer and begging me to answer their prayers.

Each smiling face rests next to a torn up shred of paper holding a name written in fading ink. My hand brushes against the paper, ruffling it, as I find a face I recognize.

James Malhoon, his name reads. And I know him. I've worked beside him on the wall. I've beaten him with a sword, discarded him as inferior, never once caring where he came from or what his story was.

Next to him rests another familiar person—Tanya Reede. I never knew her name, but she lived next door to me. In the photo, she is only ten or eleven years old, but I recognize the curve of her nose and the shaggy wave of her hair. I used to watch her play outside my window, alone in her backyard surrounded by dolls. She's a few years older than me, but in another life we could have been friends. In any other city, we probably would have.

"What is this place?" I ask as my eyes continue to search, to land on familiar faces. I know some of these people. Not all of them. Very few of their names.

"The missing persons room," he says, stepping next to me, holding his hand just shy of the wall, as though it is too precious to touch. "Every rebel base has one, just in case. These are all the people we search for, all those we hope to find in Kardenia."

My eyes land on Maddy's father—there is no doubt in my mind. The full-teeth grin is exactly the same, the wide warm eyes, the excitement. There is also no doubt that I have never seen him before.

"Asher?" I ask, an idea taking hold over my mind. My pulse starts to speed. My mind whirls. "Asher, what if I'm on this wall? What if—"

He silences me with one glance. The sympathy darkening his eyes is enough to drop my spirits, to snuff any hope I might have had, however small. My mother is not with the rebels. She is not here.

"I'm sorry, Jade." He shakes his head. "I checked. As soon as we arrived, I checked, but I never found your name. It's why I wasn't going to show you this place, not ever—"

"I'm glad you did," I interrupt him. After I say the words, I realize I truly mean them. They were not empty, not voiced just to make him feel better. My heart feels lighter too. "Maddy asked me about her father, and I told her the truth—I do not know him. But there are some people here who I do remember. Some people I might be able to..." I pause, searching for the world as it catches on my tongue. "To help."

Asher's eyes land on me, sending a chill up my spine, but I don't look at him. I keep my eyes locked on the walls around us, worried what might happen if I do meet his stare.

Every word I say and every action I take seems to draw us closer together. Even now, my hairs stand upright on my forearms, reaching for his body against my will, electric in the minute space between us. We are connected somehow, and even when I try to pull away, I end up pushing closer.

But it is not right. Not when my lie still burns secret in my chest. Yet as my brain shouts to stay still, to let the moment pass, my head shifts ever so slightly toward him.

Closer.

Closer.

Until...

A shatter echoes against the walls. Glass breaks, cracking against stone, sending a shock wave up my body.

I jump, reaching for an invisible knife at my hip as I turn. Old habits die hard. But there is no need. No enemy waits, no soldier, no rebel with a gun.

Just an old woman.

Flowers circle her feet as water spreads, filling the cracks in the stone, funneling toward us. Shards are all that remain of the vase that rested in her hands, which now grasp empty space. I didn't notice the other bouquets before, but they line the base of the wall, some dried and brittle, others fresh and silky.

Asher speeds into action, flying toward the woman, crouching down to save her petals from wilting against the ground.

"Are you all right?" He asks while handing them back to her. The roses are dripping wet but safe.

She nods, taking them, and Asher begins to work on the glass, scooping it into a pile in the corner.

I don't move.

Her gaze has caught mine and we stand, opposite one another, just staring. I can't read her expression. I don't understand what she sees in my eyes.

"You're the prisoner?" she asks, voice still like the wind, barely there.

I sway on my feet, anxious, as my hands wring behind my back. "Yes."

The woman steps closer, ignoring Asher as her feet carry her forward. In the light, shadows line her face, wrinkled grooves that reveal her age.

"But you're just a child," she says, barely a foot away. "No older than my grandson."

"Old enough to fight and get caught." I shrug, uncomfortable under her scrutiny, unused to being questioned about my age.

The woman seems to accept that, though a frown flattens her lips, and she steps past me.

"My husband turns seventy-six today," she tells me, and I notice that she uses the present tense, unfalteringly loyal.

"Is his picture on the wall?"

"Here."

She points and I follow her slow steps to the left, until her finger lands on a photograph. Her movement is graceful as she bends down, arranging the flowers at the base of the wall, perfectly centered on his image as though she has done it before. And she has. For more than a decade.

The old man in the picture is not familiar to me, but I like his smile. He seems to be laughing, to be happy.

I remain silent. I don't want to dash her hopes.

"My daughter was a pilot." Her voice is soothing, like a lullaby, warm and gentle. "Her plane fell from the sky during the first attacks. She was trying to save her son. His grandpa had taken him into the city for the afternoon, to the zoo in Central Park, when the earthquake hit. I don't think she ever forgave herself for being with me when it happened, complaining about his father, worrying over their divorce."

A long sigh escapes her lips and her finger shifts a few inches to the side, to the photograph of a little boy.

A little boy I know very well.

"Brock," I say unintentionally—the word pops out just as surprised as I am. We were in the same training group. I have punched his face too many times not to recognize it. His grin does not seem so smug on a child, but I know the teenager, the guard who worked beside me on the wall, chiding me like all the other boys.

Weak fingers clutch my arm, and I realize the

woman's grip is as tight as she can make it. "You know him?"

"We work together."

I catch her before she falls, using my strength to carry her weight, to keep her upright on her feet.

"He's alive," she whispers.

Saying it out loud gives her strength, so I repeat the words. "Your grandson is alive. He's a member of the queen's guard. Very strong. A good fighter."

I open my mouth to say more, but nothing comes to mind. Though I've stood next to this boy for years, manning the wall, walking through the old city, I know nothing about him. I've never even seen his grandfather. Do they live together? Does Brock even know the man is alive? Does he remember him?

As I speak, she lets go of me, brushing her finger lightly against his baby picture. I hastily think of more to say.

"He's a good man." I settle on those words, not completely sincere but not wrong either. Brock can be lazy, and he says things that sting, but he is no worse than the rest of them, and right now I want to bring this woman peace.

Her eyes glisten, wet with unshed tears.

"I'm sorry," I apologize. I've made her upset. I don't understand how.

"No, child," she hushes, shaking her head as the

droplets finally fall, dipping in and out of the grooves on her cheeks before slipping to the floor. "These are tears of joy."

The woman turns back to the picture, eyes bright and glued to her grandson. I watch for a moment, then look away, uncomfortable as though I'm intruding on something I shouldn't.

The eyes around me turn judging.

The photographs close in, accusing, as though they know why I'm really here. As if they know it was not by accident that I find myself in the rebel camp.

You're my enemy, they shout, cutting like knives because it is the truth. I fight on the wall. I fight for the queen.

I thought I fought to keep the rebels out, but now I see past the façade. I fought to keep these people in, to keep them locked in their prison, to keep them away from the families that yearn for them.

Without looking back, I run from the room.

"Jade!" Asher shouts after me.

I don't slow down. I keep sprinting. The halls all look the same, and I take them at random, not knowing where I'm going but not caring. I just need to get as far away from that room as possible, as far away from those photographs as I can.

"Take a left," Asher calls, sarcasm heavy in his panting voice.

I listen.

A familiar door springs into view, and I realize that somehow I've found my way back to my cage.

Good.

I deserve to be locked up.

Asher grabs my hand, sliding his fingers into mine, turning me around before I can step inside. With his other hand, he cups my cheek, forcing me to meet his eyes.

How can two people who look so alike be so different? The queen is etched in his face, his straight nose, his pale skin, his almost white hair. But all those angles seem soft, smooth, not harsh like hers. And in his eyes, the universe waits for me, almost within reach.

How can the woman who owns me have a son so determined to set me free?

"You were amazing."

I edge back from his touch, from his words. I do not want praise, not now.

"Can you take me there tomorrow?" I ask, breaking contact, feeling cold the minute his skin leaves mine.

"Sure." He watches me, confused, pulling his arms back to his side, dropping them there, lifeless.

I've wounded him. I don't have time to feel sorry. My throat itches and my nose burns, sensations that have become familiar. And this time, I need to sob in isolation. I do not deserve the feel of warm arms around me, not when I have worked so hard to keep warm arms away from other people.

"Bring a pen and paper," I tell him and then I am gone, hidden behind the door just as my legs give out and I fall, overcome with emotions I am unused to.

My head lands just behind the door, and I see Asher's feet under the crack, still outside of my room. He waits and I'm sure he can hear me though I try to cry as silently as possible.

Eventually, he gives in.

Through blurry eyes, I watch his shadow disappear.

Fourteen

When Asher arrives the next day, I am the strong Jade again. I have promised myself that there will be no more tears, that I will not waste my time feeling sorry when I can spend it correcting my mistakes.

We walk silently to the missing persons room, hands a few inches apart—a distance that consumes my thoughts the entire way there.

Asher is different. He is solemn, quiet, something I have never seen from him. And in the silence, words escape me. My lips feel awkward. They open to speak, but each time, I stop and close them again, unsure. I squirm in my own skin, uncomfortable. I hurt him, but I don't know how, so I also don't know how to fix it.

When we reach the photographs, we both stop. I lick my lips, unable to avoid conversation any longer.

"I'm sure you're wondering why I wanted to come back, when I left so hastily yesterday..." I trail off as Asher nods. I wait until I realize he does not want to speak. "Anyway, I thought we could go through each picture and write down if I know the person, if they are alive, maybe a little about their life in Kardenia. I can't speak with everyone, not like yesterday, but maybe this would still help."

"It will," he says, tone not giving anything away. Then he sits, resting the notebook in his lap with a pen at the ready.

I take it as my cue to continue and for the next few hours, nothing changes except my position in the room.

I start at the left side, making my way through each and every photograph, telling Asher how much or little I know about these people. Most are foreign to me, some I recognize from passing glances, some I've actually interacted with, and a rare few like Brock are truly familiar to me.

The only sound aside from my voice is the constant scratching of the pen. Asher barely looks up from the paper, barely watches me. I feel as though something between us snapped, recoiled, and will never connect again.

But I try my best to ignore it, to remain strong even as my throat dries and my voice cracks. I push through, until finally my gaze is on the opposite wall, on the final photo. A woman I've never seen before. One of the many I cannot help.

With a sigh, I roll my shoulders and turn around. Though I'm tired, a new sort of energy fills my stomach.

Satisfaction. A warm glow filters through my veins, brings a smile to my face.

Am I happy?

I can't be sure, but my body is lighter, more buoyant. Not quite like Maddy, but there is an electric charge running through my system that I've never felt before.

"All done?" Asher asks. He sounds exhausted, as though it is more than just physical, as though a tiredness fills his mind as well. Slowly, he stands, stretching stale muscles and slipping the notebook back into his pocket. "I'll share the news, tell everyone what you've told me."

"Thank you," I say, and then we slip into silence. The terrible kind. Not the sort of quiet that lets the mind sit at peace, not the silence we had when he held me, when he comforted me as my tears continued to fall.

This silence is a wall rising between us, separating us—a new dividing line, one that scares me now that I know what it's like to be on the same side of the threshold. None of my words can break through, and the longer it exists, the more distant we become. My body stings, prickled with an anxious nervousness I've never felt in his presence before.

Asher leaves and I follow behind him, not even trying to catch up. We make our way through the maze like ghosts until he delivers me back to my room. Then we stand, eyes trapped, throats empty, in a trance.

He looks away, starts to turn, but I know I cannot leave it like this. If we don't speak now, I'm worried we never will again, that whatever was between us will be irreparable, broken, gone forever.

And I know I should let him go. That in the end he will be better for it. But I've lost so much already.

I'm a statue, frozen, so unsure.

His back is to me now. His feet rise to walk away.

"Asher!" I shout. The words are expelled with more force than I realize. A tremor runs through his body, a pause, but then he moves forward again. So I reach with my hand, grabbing his fingers as I've wanted to all day, forcing him to turn around.

Pain fills his eyes.

"Asher, what is wrong?" The awkward air has dissipated. It was pushed away, replaced by something more demanding. My gut needs to understand.

"It's nothing, Jade."

But I refuse to accept that, and I tug on his arm, bringing him fully around to face me.

"Asher." My voice is low and unrelenting. Chiding even.

Obstinate, he remains silent.

"Asher, what did I do?"

Finally his face cracks, brows furrowing as his entire body hunches. "You didn't do anything, Jade. Really. It's not about you, it's…" He looks around, examining the hallway, and I realize what it's about.

His mother. The queen.

No other topic would consume him so much, no other person. And no one in the rebel camp knows of his true lineage, which is why he is nervously scanning the perimeter, searching for overeager ears.

But he can talk to me.

So without warning, I yank forcefully on his arm, throwing him off balance so he stumbles into my room. Before he has a chance to right himself, I close the door, standing before it, doing what I do best—guarding.

We are alone. Shut off from the world. And it will stay that way until I get the truth from him.

"Tell me," I demand.

Confliction flickers in his squint, his pursed lips, the way he shakes as he runs a hand through his hair. Then it disappears in one long exhale that smoothes the tension from his body, dropping his shoulders, straightening his spine.

"How did you know I'm the prince?"

I stop, twitch, wondering how many truths are about to be revealed.

"Everyone in the guard knows," I say slowly, choosing every word with caution.

A knowing smile, an empty one, crosses his lips. "You were supposed to capture me on that first day, right? To bring me back to the queen? To my mother?"

I nod, afraid of what I might give away.

"It's okay, I don't blame you. As soon as you told me

you knew who I am, I guessed as much. That's not what bothers me. It's the why."

"Why what?"

"Why she wants me back."

"Because you're her son," I say. It's a gut reaction, an automatic response.

Asher laughs darkly, under his breath. "Right, because I'm her son. Her only child."

There is a deeper meaning there but I don't understand.

"I look at that wall of photographs, and I see a hundred people who want their families back, who miss them, who love them. And I know no such shrine waits for me back home. My mother doesn't put flowers out on my birthday. She doesn't visit my old room, wondering what became of her lost child. She doesn't imagine what the years have made me look like."

He's right, but I don't say so. I don't want to hurt him, not when he looks so fragile already.

"She doesn't want me back because she loves me. She wants me back so she can use me."

"Asher." I reach my hand out, squeezing his shoulder. I can't go so far as to deny it—the queen does not know love. But still, there is something in his words I cannot see, a hidden meaning that is beyond me. A secret only he and his mother share.

"I've accepted it," he tells me, whispers, as his gaze

lifts to meet my eyes. "But I thought someday, somehow, someone else might want me. Might want to love me. I thought..."

His eyes drop to my lips.

A lightning bolt flares down my spine, hot and electric, standing my every nerve on end. We are close enough to touch. Heat seeps into my hand, lifting from his skin and coursing into my body.

Our eyes meet again.

Asher breaks away, stepping out of my hold. I want to follow, to bring him back, but I am stuck as a wave of cold water washes over me, hurts me, leaves me wounded.

"Magic always starts with a curse, that's what we used to say back in my world. And it does." He breathes deeply, raw, and I know I am staring into his soul. I watch all the layers he has built come crashing down, melt to the floor, until all that remains is a basic fear, the sort that every person secretly holds in their hearts, buried in doubts.

"I am cursed. So was my mother. And her mother before her. We all yearn for love, ache for it, but we never find it. And that's why we have the magic, so we can take the love no one will ever willingly give us. And I fear..." He shutters, a shake that ripples down his frame. "I fear that one day I'll be just like her."

"You won't," I urge, but he looks away.

I step closer, put my palm against his warm cheek, and bring his face back to mine. My thumb runs along the groove of his jaw, back to his ear as my fingers slip through the short hairs at the base of his neck.

"Asher, you won't."

This time he does not try to look away, but I can see he does not believe me. He has faith, it seems, in everyone but himself.

"How do you know?" he whispers. "No one in Kardenia misses me. No one here would put my face on the wall if I disappeared. No one would care, not really, not like with their families."

I step closer. Our toes touch. Our hips just barely brush against each other. My free hand finds his, our fingers clench, holding on for life.

"I would," I murmur.

There is a truth buried in the deep indigo of his eyes. It pulls me in, binds us.

We were meant to save each other.

And then his lips are on mine and I can't think any longer. My thoughts evaporate. Fire burns them all away. Flames that spark at my mouth then grow as they travel down into my chest, along my arms, to the very tips of my toes.

Asher pushes me back until I hit the wall, and then he presses further, until every inch of us touches, burns. His leg comes between mine as my hands clasp behind his neck, urging him closer. Hands grip my waist, just skimming my bare skin, pulling me toward him.

Time stops as we seem to fly, to soar together. I forget the cell, the room, the rebel camp. I forget that we are underground, because behind my closed eyes all I see are stars. The ones that spark in his irises, the ones that I've stared at for years on the wall. Stars and open skies and freedom.

That's the promise in his lips. The tantalizing dream that makes me pull on his shoulders, that makes him lift me up so my heels leave the ground and he holds me, arms crushing behind my back.

And I am lost there. Drowning in these sensations that my body has never experienced. In a warmth I thought my frozen soul would never find. My heart swells so that it might burst. And down in the depths of my mind, a damn breaks.

A curse lifts.

I stop moving as shock works its way through my system, stilling me, opening my eyes wide. Asher does the same, as though his shackles have shattered too.

Our breath comes ragged, uneven, heaving.

I blink, vision slowly returning as I sink back down to earth, but eternity still shines in his eyes.

"So…" he whispers. There is an excitement in his tone that I missed, that I thought was gone.

"So…" I copy, surprised to hear that my voice carries an electricity of its own. Something new. Something I like.

Time stretches as we communicate without words,

lights dance in the space between us, sparking, talking for us.

But then it goes on too long, just a hair, just a bit. A nervous tingle shivers up my spine. My lips start to bend. I purse them, trying to hold this sudden outburst in. But I can't, and giggles leak out.

Happy.

Foreign to my ears.

Asher's deep laugh follows, spurns me on until my whole body is shaking, but I cannot stop even if I wanted to. Our hands reach for each other, holding us up as our legs start to give out, and our bodies lose control in a completely different sort of way.

We fall.

I laugh even harder, curling into his chest as his arms come around me, hold me.

After a while, the sound fades, bringing back the comfortable silence I am used to. I listen to his heartbeat slow, his breath even, and I shift just slightly so I am above his face, looking down at him.

A sigh escapes his lips, content, but also resigned.

"I should get these notes to the general, so he can make copies for people to read."

"Okay," I murmur, still in a daze.

Quickly, he lifts his face, lips brushing mine for just an instant, too fast for me to even realize until they are gone, far away.

He smiles, eyes bright as they watch me watch him.

"I'll be back soon."

And then he stands, but I don't make a move to follow. My limbs are jelly. I don't know if they work anymore.

Before he leaves, Asher bends down, placing one last quick kiss on my lips. As he pulls away, my face follows, stretches higher.

After he is gone, I sit for I don't know how long, fingers touching my swollen lips, wondering if the entire memory was a dream.

When my strength returns, I slide over to my books in the corner, pulling out the one with pictures, flipping to the end where my missing pages have been torn free.

I don't need them. Not anymore.

Asher didn't say and yet I know now how the story ends. With a kiss. The prince wakes the princess with a kiss, ending her slumber, bringing her back to life, making her broken heart beat again.

Mine thumps in my chest.

Hot.

Melting all the ice away.

Fifteen

The next time Asher knocks on my door, I spring to life. Every nerve in my body ignites, alert, waiting and anticipating what will come next. When the door creaks open, my gaze lands on his face and sparks explode in my chest. Tingles filter out to my fingers, slide into my stomach, a fluttering swarm of excitement.

"Hey," he says, leaning against the doorframe, smile wide and goofy. Though I can't see it, I know my cheeks are pulled into a similar expression. Instinctually.

"Hey."

My brain doesn't seem to be working, because I can't think of anything else to say. I'm too consumed by the shape of his lips, the curve of his hair as it swoops just slightly over his eyes, the way his muscles push gently against the fabric of his shirt.

Is this what emotions do? Take away control. Take away reason.

My body buzzes, alive, yet my mind lays just beyond reach. My lips prickle from my memories of the day before, filled with a need that takes my thoughts away.

I'm delirious. Drunk.

Like an addict, I want more.

Asher speaks but I don't register the words.

"Huh?" I look up, eyes finally finding his, pulled from my explorations. His pupils darken, eyes narrowing slyly. I know he's guessed my thoughts.

"I said, do you want to get out of here? I think we should go on a date."

"A date?" I cross my arms, eyebrow raised. "Where?"

Talking is helping. My speech is coming back. My attitude is too.

"It's a surprise."

"I thought I wasn't allowed to leave, being a prisoner and everything."

Asher just rolls his eyes. And he's right. This room doesn't feel like a cell, I don't feel like a hostage, not anymore. "Come on, you've got to trust me. You'll love this."

"Trust you?" I say, exaggerated, just to push his buttons. Asher grabs my hand, sending a thrill down my spine, and pulls me toward him. I land against his chest.

"Yeah, trust me," he whispers.

For a moment, I think he might kiss me, but then he steps away, bringing me into the hallway with him.

I go willingly. Because I do trust him, no matter how much that idea scares me. The queen seems far away and so do the promises I made her. They're lost in the wind, and I'm happy to watch them disappear.

Voices grow louder the farther we walk, reverberating down the hall. Laughter. Conversation. High pitched excitement that intrigues me.

When we turn a corner, I'm presented with a huge room filled to the brim with people. They sit on blankets, on pillows and cushions, all along the floor, filling every nook. At the far wall, a huge white screen is pulled taught, tied to hooks in the concrete.

"What?" I start to ask, but Asher does not stop, and we keep making our way through the crowd, carefully stepping around people, over their blankets, steering clear of any wayward fingers.

We don't stop until we reach the corner of the back wall, and then Asher produces a blanket of his own, spreading it across the floor and sitting. Opening his arm wide, he looks up, nodding at me.

"I just wanted to get a good spot," he says, leaning back against the wall.

Still confused, I slowly sit. Asher's arm comes around my shoulders, and I shift back until my head rests against his, and our bodies mold together.

"What's going on?"

"You'll see," Asher prods.

"Can't you just tell me?" I ask, already anticipating his answer, which is a shrug and a firm, "Nope."

I sigh, annoyed, and look away from his smirk.

My gaze searches the room, watching other people settle in. Little children rest on adult laps, couples hold hands, lean against each another like Asher and me. The entire room is connected by a sense of familiarity. People smiling at one another, waving hello, catching up. There's a warmth among these strangers that I've never felt before, a glow that bonds them.

I spot Maddy across the room with a boy our age and we smile at each other, her eyes contracting in question as she takes note of Asher. Then she winks and I bite my lip, shaking my head slightly. No doubt she'll be paying me a visit soon. But I don't mind.

Other eyes soon find me around the room. Inviting. Shy. Suggesting a hello and maybe a thank you, but no one comes over to say anything. Still, a tenderness lodges in my stomach, suggesting that maybe I've found somewhere I belong.

The conversation is growing softer, gently muting as though everyone knows what is about to happen, and knows that they must be silent. I keep quiet too, even as Asher places a gentle kiss on the back of my neck, zapping my senses to life.

The lights dim, blanketing everyone in shadow.

Then I gasp.

Asher squeezes me tighter against him, enjoying the sight of my shock. But right before my eyes, pictures move along the screen. Colors flare to life, music fills the room.

"It's called a movie," he whispers.

A movie. I know the term. Remember them, almost. Images from a past life filter before my eyes, a small television in the living room, my mother brushing my hair as I sang along to whatever played on the screen.

I snuggle closer to Asher, enjoying how warm his skin feels against mine, how nice his fingers feel as they brush my upper arm, caressing me. My hand finds its way to the ripples of his hard abs as I curl onto my side, and he holds it so our fingers can dance, silky smooth as they weave in and out, touching then pulling away only to find each other again.

The movie starts with a girl on a farm, black and white, until a great tornado carries her away, takes her to a majestic world full of color. That is how I feel. Swept away in a dream, to world brighter than I realized it could be—more full, more vibrant, more alive. Every breath is more purposeful. Every smile holds more meaning. Every touch more powerful.

But unlike the girl, I don't want to leave. She yearns to go home, but I feel like maybe I've finally found it. I never realized what my old life was missing, but now I can't go back. I don't want to let go.

And that scares me.

Perhaps I've lived without emotion for too long, but I know these feelings can't last forever. That they won't. I'm dangling from the edge of a steep cliff, holding on for as long as possible, but eventually I'll fall.

My time is running out.

The rebels are planning something, are planning to act. Otherwise why take me? Why venture into the city at all? And the queen knows it, which is why she sent me here to mess with their plan.

I'm in the middle. Stuck. Caught.

When the lights turn back on and the closing credits fill the screen, panic alarms my system, makes me tremble.

"Jade?" Asher asks, clutching my hand, trying to still the quiver. His tone is concerned, worried.

I turn my head, looking up at him, and I know my eyes are wide, pulled taut, slightly crazed. "I don't want to go back to my room, not yet."

I don't want the night to end. Somehow, it suddenly feels like it is the last one we have left. My heart pounds. And though I know it's insane, that my mind is running wild, I cannot stop it. My emotions are a rollercoaster I cannot slow, that I don't know how to anticipate.

"Okay," he tells me, brushing my cheek one time, before we ease apart and up. Asher folds the blanket, abandoning it in the corner before taking my hand again. I'm paralyzed without his touch, lost in my frantic pulse. "I know just the place, come on."

A slanted grin lights his face, a sneaky smile that warms me, slows the rapid beating until it has changed just slightly, not so nervous and more excited. A fine line I'm happy to cross.

"I would ask where we're going, but I'm guessing you won't tell me."

"Nope." Asher shakes his head.

I've never been one for surprises, until now. The thrill of not knowing is intoxicating, and as we leave the crowd behind, choosing different hallways, I find myself growing more intrigued.

The silence is thick. Voices have drifted away, leaving only the scuff of our boots against the floor, the puff of our breath. We seem to be drifting higher. My thighs begin to burn with the angle of our steps until we reach a dead end.

Asher looks back once, checking on my reaction, expectant. And then he starts climbing a ladder I did not notice, only ten or fifteen rungs. At the top, a circle waits unopened.

My throat catches.

"Are we…?"

I drift off as his hand grasps a handle I can hardly make out, and then the stars fill my vision. The midnight blue sky. The shadow of trees.

The outside.

"Asher," I gasp, jumping to the ladder and letting him pull me up through the hole as I reach the top.

A cold breeze licks my cheeks, ruffles my hair, and I sigh, content. I smell grass and dirt, fresh air. I hear crickets. We are in an open field patched with trees. Behind us, large shadowy houses loom, and before us it looks clear. Above me, the moon shines bright, almost full, casting a luminescent glow over Asher's pale skin, making him seem almost more than human.

My skin was made for the sun, the caramel hue is made warmer, the gold in my jade eyes shines brighter. But Asher was made for the night. His eyes sparkle with reflections from the stars, dark and mysterious, tantalizing.

"I..."

But I stop. My confession burns my lips, and I hold it in. I want to tell him about my promise to the queen, my mission to betray him, but the perfection of the moment stops me. The longer I wait, the worse his reaction will be, the more betrayed he will feel, but we've already come too far it seems. How can I turn back now?

As I watch him, I know that he broke through the queen's thrall. When he ran away as a boy, he escaped her hold. He managed to overcome. And it gives me hope, a feeling I've never really had before. With his help, I can fight her. When we kissed, I felt the curse disappear.

Maybe he will never have to know.

"I think you need to have a little fun," Asher says. I swallow the confession back down, bury it deep in my stomach. I will not ruin this night.

"What did you have in mind?"

"Just a little something," he casually drawls on, "see if you can keep up."

And then Asher is gone, sprinting away, and I'm stopped with surprise. But not a second later, I chase after him.

My legs pump, awakening old muscles, stretching them, using my body in a way that I've missed. I sink back into the motions easily. Years of jogging the perimeter of the wall have trained me well, and Asher is no match.

I tap his shoulder as I pass him by, laughing as his eyes open wide with shock. My head is turned for a second too long, and I watch him dip low, pushing harder than he thought he would have too. I face forward again, determined to outrun him. I've been outpacing boys for my entire life, what's one more?

The longer we run, the better I feel. My legs grow stronger, faster, and the world begins to blur around me.

"Alright," Asher's faint voice shouts from behind me, "I give up."

I turn around, light on my feet, only to see him bent at the waist, doubled over. I bite my lips, trying to keep controlled as I walk back. But these new emotions are unruly, hard to hide.

"I hear you snickering," Asher accuses. I can't even deny it. He looks up from the grass, eyebrows raised, ready to refute any argument I make. "I'll admit, this isn't going quite how I planned. You were supposed to lose, admiring my backside the entire way there, completely overwhelmed by my awesomeness. You were not supposed to strip me of my dignity."

"Sorry." I shrug. "But I wasn't about to let you win."

"I see." Asher pauses, eyes narrowing as his head fills with an idea. Something I'm not sure I'll like. "Let's try something else then."

And before I can move, his arms surround my thighs, lifting me into the air so my torso falls over his shoulder. I have nowhere to stare except the curve of his butt and the grassy floor, which seems a little far away and not nearly as interesting.

"Asher!" I kick my feet, but he won't let go. In fact, I'm the one who hears him snicker now. "Put me down."

"I don't think so," he says and starts walking forward. "I should have just done this from the beginning," he mutters to himself, "why in the world did I think I could outrun you?"

I roll my eyes. "Because boys always think they can beat me, and I always prove them wrong. Now put me down, or—"

"Or what?" His tone is light, musical, and full of different chimes.

Below me, the grass starts to thin. Dirt pokes through, becoming thicker, until even those disappear to what looks like wooden slabs, striped in the moonlight.

"Asher," I warn.

To either side of the planks rests velvet black, shimmering just slightly from the stars.

"What?" he asks, far too innocent.

"Don't you dare."

"Well, when you put it like that…" He stops, shifts my weight, only pretending to set me down. His hands have inched up to my waist, gripping my hipbones.

"Ash—" But the word disappears into a scream as I'm flung airborne with a strength I didn't realize his arms possessed. The water prickles my skin, ice-cold, as I crash against the surface, sinking deep before my arms and legs jump into action, swimming for air.

I take a deep gulp before I shriek, "Asher, you're dead!" My arms sliver through the liquid, back to the dock where I pull myself up and out, back to the pier. My eyes search through the darkness, needing to readjust after my sink into ebony, and I can't find him.

Alert, I walk back to the shore.

Movement flashes on my left and I turn, mouth dropping as Asher swings by me, zipping through the air on a rope, releasing at the peak to drop with a loud splash into the lake.

"What?" I'm laughing. I can't help it, my anger has disappeared, replaced with a bubbly joy.

He surfaces with an excited shout. "Come on, your turn. I said we were going to have some fun tonight."

I nod, forgetting he can't see, and catch the swinging rope in my hand. The texture is coarse against my skin, and I follow the line until I can make out the large knot tied at the bottom, an anchor for my feet.

"Just go for it," Asher calls from the darkness, sensing my hesitation. It's hard for me to let go, but knowing he waits to catch me, I give in.

Stepping back slowly, I go as far as the rope allows. Taking a deep breath, I jump, released from the ground, hands burning as they grip the twine and my feet struggle to locate the knot.

Secure, I rush toward the ground, worried that the rope will snap, but it doesn't. My body arches up, swings higher, and just as a weightlessness takes hold, I let go, soaring farther, laughter caught by the wind, and then I drop below the surface.

Hands snake around my waist under the water, hot despite the chill, and when I emerge, Asher waits for me, face close so our noses are less than an inch away from touching.

Our eyes meet and time stops. My heart stops beating. My mind instantly clears. All I see is him, us, in this moment. This perfect moment. Fleeting as it may be, it's ours, and no one, not even the queen, can take it away. The urgency I felt before returns, boils my blood, makes my skin buzz. I want to hold on to this moment forever, I don't want it to end.

My hands rise to his cheeks, and I pull his face to mine, closing the gap until our lips crush together, hungry. I drink him in, never satisfied, aching for more.

We sink below the surface, arms entangled. My legs wrapped around his waist, and all I can think is that if this is a dream, I don't ever want to wake up.

Sixteen

The next morning, I jolt from my slumber, heart in my throat, fighting the urge to scream.

The queen.

She is watching me. Icy blue eyes haunt my dreams, bare my soul, sift through my thoughts as though they belong to her. I try to still my beating heart, to calm my pulse, but it is of no use.

"Jade?"

I yelp, stomach lunging into my throat, but it is just Asher. His eyes are still half closed in sleep, his voice is airy. Slowly, he adjusts on the bed, hand searching for mine. I can't tell if he is asleep or awake, but I move my fingers so they find his.

As our skin touches, memories shake the nightmare away, and I relive the lake. The cool water that almost sizzled against our flaming skin. I remember coming back to my room afterward, talking, kissing. We fell asleep on top of the covers and still in our clothes. The room smells like moss, as though we brought the outdoors inside, and now that I am not within Asher's embrace, my skin feels cool in clothes that are still damp.

I hug myself, fighting shivers that are sure to come. I've grown unused to the chill, but now the sensation is flooding back.

Was it just a nightmare?

Or did the queen visit me in my sleep?

I've never had a nightmare before, not that I can remember, but I decide that is what it must have been. Neurosis. A scare. I push the queen from my mind, determined to leave her behind.

Asher adjusts again, sinking the bed with our weight, and his eyes begin to blink open. I watch as they clear. When they recognize my features, his entire face relaxes, glows.

"Morning," I mutter, soft.

"Morning," he whispers. But then his body tenses, eyes going wide. "Morning?"

"I think." I shrug. The artificial lights are still difficult for me to read, but my body feels rested, as though hours have passed and the night is long behind us.

Asher leaps from the bed in one long bound.

"I'll be back in ten minutes, okay?"

He leaves before I can gather a response, zipping from my room and closing the door behind him.

Mute, I slide from the bed, still confused. But my skin itches against the wet clothes, scratching raw, so I change into soft worn jeans and a large sweater. By the time I have curled my hair into an unruly bun, Asher is back.

"Is everything okay?" I ask, opening the door to greet a far more composed prince.

"Yeah, we're just late." He grabs my hand and our fingers entwine, naturally.

"For what?"

"To meet General Willis." Asher grins at my reaction. "He wants to talk to you, to show you some things."

A general of the rebellion wants to speak with me? My mouth goes dry. I should have expected this, seen it coming. I am, after all, a valuable prisoner. But still. Weeks ago, I yearned to put a knife in this man's chest. Now, I want to impress him.

We take a few long corridors, ones I am sure I have not yet traversed, until we reach a large metal door sealed with a circular wheel. One tug, and the door swings open easily, proving just how safe the rebels feel in their underground haven. The locks aren't even being used.

But I forget that thought quickly as my eyes take in the scene before me. The room is blinking, small bulbs turn on and off, switchboards display lines that disappear and reappear each second. A big screen illuminates a map, unlike any I have beheld in the books I've studied. Men and women sit with large headpieces encasing their ears, typing on keyboards that I have only before seen coated in dust.

I now know what most of the solar electricity they gather is used for. The gadgets are beyond me, and I do not understand their uses, but I know without a doubt that the purpose of this room is defense.

"Asher," a deep voice booms.

A large man walks forward, taller than me, taller even than the commander. His clothes are spotted different shades of green, and the word *Willis* is stitched onto his chest. The general.

"Jade, I assume?" He extends his hand and I take it, gripping hard. The skin around his eyes is wrinkled, his back hunches just slightly. Though he is imposing, his prime years have come and gone already.

"General Willis." I nod, unsure of what else to say.

"Jade, welcome to the northeastern command center. Ground zero in the fight against Queen Deirdre, one of the many freedom fighter bases around the world."

Years of training come flooding back to my system, and I straighten my stance, bringing my feet together and elongating my spine until I am as tall as I can be. My voice grows even, controlled. "Happy to be here, sir."

"Are you?"

He leans in, peering deep into my eyes, and I swallow. This man does not trust me. So I glance around, noticing other stares, some blatant, some peripheral, and I understand that no one in the room trusts me either.

I am still the enemy in here.

"I am," I respond, no hint of hurt in my words, "and I would like to help in whatever way I can."

The corner of his lip twitches. "Good."

Putting a hand at the small of my back, he leads me around the desks toward the front of the room where a map of Kardenia glows green on a tabletop. The wall, the old city, the broken down skyscrapers, the castle. Everything is outlined there, but immediately I also notice that parts of it are wrong.

I open my mouth, but close it, waiting for orders.

"Go on," he drawls, and I meet his gaze only to see amusement on his features, as though my attempt at control entertains him.

"It's nothing." I bite my lip, then breathe. "It's just the layout of the wall is not correct. Most of Kardenia is outlined well, and the old city too, but the wall..." I shake my head, leaning over the map, using my fingers to show him the differences. "The south section is where I normally work, and it's about a hundred yards lower than where you've placed it. These streets here fill out into dead ends, and then we have practice grounds on the inner loop of the wall, and the entrance gate has been moved closer to the west side of the city."

"Drew, are you recording all of this?"

I follow the general's eyes to a man a few feet to the left of me, hunched over his computer and furiously typing.

A nod is his only response and then a few moments later the screen blinks and my changes have been implemented.

"Can I?" I pause, waiting until the general gives me permission, "Can I ask how you knew all of this already?"

"Asher," General Willis tells me, looking over our shoulders to where Asher waits patiently by the door, not stepping too far into the room, but watching us. He grins as our gazes meet. A thrill travels up my back, but I quickly turn to the map as the heat reaches my cheeks. "When he first arrived as a boy, he told us everything he could remember about his former home. We cross-matched his descriptions against old maps of New York. Pretty good, right?"

I smirk my consent, and then continue talking about Kardenia, describing the layout of the streets, different buildings that have been changed since they last gathered information. The northern side is all farmland, empty and open, a difficult place to hide. So we move onto the old city, and I give them the exact locations of our mines, which streets we have cleared out and will be the easiest to traverse, and also the areas we know are too fragile to walk upon.

My stomach is completely at ease as I give the guard's secrets away, as I betray everyone from my former life, as I work against the queen. In fact, my body relaxes the more I speak.

Betrayal, it seems, comes naturally to me.

But I throw that thought aside, sparing a glance at Asher who watches me with a satisfied expression, in a way that makes me think he might almost be proud.

"That's everything I can think of." I lean back, hands at my waist, scanning my brain for any other morsel of information. But I come up blank.

A beefy hand lands on my shoulder. "That was great," the general tells me. And I believe him. Though he might seem like the commander, this man doles out praises I've never heard back home. Genuine. Kind. As I look around, I realize he is followed out of respect. A feeling I don't quite understand.

Scanning the room, I also sense that I've been dismissed. The general has turned away from me, discussing a plan I am not privy to, and the room surges back into motion. The rebels are done listening to me talk.

I'm not.

I crave more information. An entire world is depicted on the screen before me, and I want to know what waits for us out there. What my freedom might really mean. My mind wanders to my paintings, to the gardens of France, the canals of Venice, the rainforest of the Amazon. Are they still there?

"Can we ever go back?" I ask aloud, unintentionally.

"No, Jade." Is the general's soft reply. Maybe he hadn't dismissed me after all.

He steps closer, following my stare to the large map flashing on the front wall, to a world forever changed. The continents look different, are narrow where they should be wide, long where they should be short. Islands sprout in oceans that were once vast.

A red dot depicts our location, and directly north of it is a large hazy circle where no details can be seen. All around the world, more misty circles interrupt clean shorelines, and I know that is the magic. The electric instruments in this room cannot penetrate the aura it holds, so those areas are menacingly vacant, are unknown.

"No one really knows why or how the merge happened. Cindy over there," he says, pointing to a woman scrawling on paper, bent over her desk, "is our resident physicist. Ask her, and she'll bore you to death with string theory, quantum mechanics, long words none of us normal people understands. But the best guess we have is that the magic world was running parallel to our own—the animals are similar, the plant life, the atmosphere. Then somehow, one of us got pushed off course, and boom," he exclaims, slapping his hands together, loud enough to shock a few people around us, "hello earthquake, hello two worlds becoming one."

"And they can't be separated?"

He shakes his head.

"Then why fight?"

"Why not?" He shrugs. "We can't change the past, but we can shape the future. Asher!"

The shout catches me off guard, and I jolt. But Asher walks over now that he's been called. His eyes are also on the map, and I realize that he still isn't completely comfortable in this room either.

"Sir?" He inquires, and I bite down a laugh, listening to Asher act so formal.

"Tell Jade what you told us all those years ago."

His eyes darken, retreating into his memories. "My world wasn't always the way it is now. The magic used to live in the sky and the earth, providing little miracles to the populace in ways unseen. It wasn't harnessed for individual use, but all of that changed hundreds of years ago. A king found a way to absorb the magic, to contain it within his body and use it for his own desires. Other monarchs discovered this and did the same, until all of the magic in our world was bottled up in royal families."

Asher pauses, glancing at me and wetting his lips, hesitant. He is about to reveal a secret he does not wish me to know, one of the few he has been hiding.

"But the magic came with consequences the royals didn't realize, with curses laid down upon generations of their families, and the power was addictive. In order to preserve their bloodlines and their reigns, the magic became transferable only to a first-born heir. If a monarch dies without an heir, the magic is released back into the wilds."

I don't understand. I'm grasping at air, hating how it flows through my fingers, unattainable. I know Asher has just revealed a truth he had been concealing, I know because he will not look at me, won't meet my gaze. Instead, his face peers only at the blinking map before us, and I wonder what world he sees.

"So," the general finishes for him, "all we need to do is kill the queen and voila, the magic is released and hopefully everything goes back to normal. No more humans under her thrall. No more anti-electricity bubble. Almost like old Earth again."

"Kill the queen..." I say slowly trailing off. Kill the queen and the magic is released. But that's not right. Not quite. "But—"

I stop sharply as fingers grip my hand, squeezing tightly, pleading. My heart stops. I turn slowly, meeting Asher's strangled gaze.

Kill the queen and the magic transfers to her heir.

To Asher.

An alarm goes off in my head, pounding, ringing so loud that all of my other senses are blocked off.

He can't mean...

But he does.

All defenses down, I see the real meaning of the words in his eyes, in Asher's sorrowful, apologetic eyes. And suddenly I'm falling. My grip is loosed, I'm tumbling over the cliff, and there is nothing I can do to stop it.

When he inherits the power, Asher means to do the one thing no one else in his family ever could. To give up the power. To let it all go. To kill himself.

My fingers tighten on his.

I won't let him do it. I won't.

"Ash—" I start to plead, voice shaking as dread floods my system. But the words are cut short by an alarm blasting through the air, reverberating around the room so loud that I know the ringing is no longer just in my head.

The beeping grows closer, quicker.

Echoes drift down from above, loud booms that sound almost simultaneously, shaking the room around us.

The general has moved into motion, shouts commands, and subordinates run to do his bidding. But I am stuck. Asher is stuck. In a frenzied room, we remain alone at the center, the eye of the storm.

I have not released his fingers.

He clutches onto mine.

The alarm continues to scream, but time is halted. Everything is about to change, is about to end. I know it. We have reached the peak, Asher and I, our climb is over, our highest height has been met, and now all that remains is the drop.

So we hold onto each other, to this last moment. I remember the lake, where everything seemed so perfect, the future limitless, the possibilities endless. From now on, the course is set. Unchanging. Doomed.

The lights in the room die out, slowly fade until it is dark and the ghost of a glow remains in my eyes.

All sound stops.

All movement.

And then a crash sounds from directly above our heads, sinking through the ground, muffled but more menacing in the ebony that surrounds us.

Time rushes forward.

The moment has snapped. It's over. And I know we will never get it back.

Seventeen

The lights switch back on and it is chaos. People run in every direction, turning the machines back to life, trying to determine what waits for us above ground.

I have a guess, but I can't be certain.

"Asher!" The general's voice calls and we both turn. He charges through the crowd, face determined, and grabs Asher by the shoulders. "It's time."

"Yes, sir." Asher nods, mission completely clear to him. "How long do I have?"

"A week, no more."

I'm not sure what just transpired, but I know I cannot leave Asher alone, not now, not when I know his real plan.

So when he turns to run from the room, I follow, feet pounding down the empty halls to the same beat as his. He knows he cannot shake me, so he doesn't try. The stomping above our heads continues, shaking dusty particles free from the ceiling, and I become more certain about what waits, but push the images from my mind. I have room for only Asher. After a few silent minutes, we slow and enter a new chamber.

Weapons.

All along the walls are guns, knives, swords, even arrows. We've reached an armory, and my fingers itch to curve around the hilt of a blade, twitch to pull the trigger of a gun. I miss the fight. My muscles ache to be used.

"Jade." Asher's voice pulls me away.

I turn to him, anticipating what his next words will be. "No."

"Jade, I'm going back to Kardenia. It's too dangerous for you to come."

I raise an eyebrow. "Too dangerous? I lived there longer than you did. I know exactly what waits for me."

Asher steps closer, warm hand cupping my cheek, eyes begging me to listen to him just this once. "You only just escaped, freed yourself from my mother. You'll lose everything if you go back."

I'll lose you if I don't.

But I can't bring myself to say the words out loud. They are too bare, too raw. So I smile encouragingly, warming my features as I lift myself an inch higher, closer to his lips.

"Then it's your job to make sure I remember," I whisper just before our lips meet, soft and tender, barely grazing. When I pull away, it is Asher who digs his fingers into my hair, urging me closer. His lips are ferocious, pressing hard against mine, hungry.

Passionate.

Desperate.

My balance fails, but he holds me up, arm wrapped around my waist. And then another crash sounds, reverberates around the room, and the weapons jingle on their hooks, reminding us both that there is no time. Asher lets go and I drop back to my feet, breathless.

"I'm coming with you," I force the airy words out. "You can't stop me."

Asher pauses, squints, and then releases a prolonged exhale. "Grab whatever weapons you can. We don't know what waits for us above ground."

Another stomp booms.

I jump into action, first discarding my sweater and then replacing it with a bulletproof vest hanging on the wall. I'm back in uniform, back on the guard, and I pull out the black heart pin I had tucked into my jeans. I'm stronger when I wear it, more formidable, more ruthless. Then I strap two handguns to my hips and tuck knives into the open spaces of the vest. The far wall is lined with heavy machine guns, and I throw one over my shoulders, just in case.

When I turn, Asher looks much the same as me. Decorated in deadly metal, ready to fight. Our minds are synced. I can read the thoughts that flutter over his features.

Concern. Thrill. Trust. The same things prick my heart as well. Without words, he leaves the room, and we make our way to a ladder leading to the outside.

I wish I could run back to my room and grab the books that Asher gave me. To turn their crisp pages once more, to lose myself in the lives he chose to give me. I wish I could find Maddy, hug her goodbye, thank her for showing me how to open myself up, to be vulnerable. I wish I could visit the missing persons room, glance once more at the people I'm indebted to, the ones I need to free. I'll miss the showers, the lights, the movies. But most of all, I will miss the freedom. My stay here has been a dream. Without the sun, time felt stalled, prolonged as though I were in a perpetual sleep. Forever stretched like a promise before me.

But now I return to the outside world. To the sunrise. The sunset. The never ending passage of time, the undulation from dark to light that whispers I will never be free.

For Asher, I willingly throw myself back behind bars.

It takes a moment for my eyes to adjust to the sun, to blink away the brightness. When I do, I know the time for thought is over. Queen Deirdre grew tired of waiting for the rebels to act, of waiting for me to bring her son back. She sent us a gift to spurn the rebellion along.

Giants.

Nine monstrous beasts loom before us, taking turns slamming their fists into the ground, trying to break the rebel camp apart, to rip the dirt open and dig their way inside. The stories from the wall were correct, almost. They are not two times the size of any man—they are three. I do not know how the queen kept them contained all of these years, but now that they are released, they are feral. Grunting mouths drip with drool. Hunched backs ripple with muscles. Clawed nails tear through the grass. If they ever looked like humans, they do not now.

As soon as my feet touch the ground, I swing the gun from my back and drop into a kneel. Taking an instant to aim, I pull the trigger. My body bounces with the force of the machine, but I keep my arms steady. Nearly an entire clip is emptied before the giant's head explodes, and he comes crashing back down to the ground.

The other eight stop, wide eyes alert, searching for me.

They land.

We stare at each other and then I run, pulling a shocked Asher with me.

But they are smarter than I anticipate and they divide into two groups of four, prepared to conquer us both as we split into two different directions.

Outrunning them for very far is impossible, so I make for the trees about fifty yards away, hoping Asher is doing the same. But I cannot think about him. My body is alert, and every ounce of effort I have is focused on the fight.

The booms of large feet get closer.

I reach the trees, ducking behind a large trunk while I reload the machine gun in my hand. Barely a second has passed before I peer around my hideout, locating another head, and I fire.

Three to go.

Bullets sound in the distance, coming from more than one weapon, and my heart feels easier. Asher must be safe. The rebels have come to his aid. But for now, I'm on my own.

I reload, peeking around the corner, but the giants have disappeared. My body tightens. There is a blockage in my throat. Slowly, I take an unsteady breath and turn to the other side.

Huge eyes watch me. A smile the size of my arm waits a few feet from my hiding place, and I dodge as branches crunch behind me. I jump, narrowly escaping the giant's fingers, and roll deeper in the trees, shooting blindly behind me. I hear a groan, knowing some bullets hit their mark. But it was stupid. My heart is in my chest, thumping wildly. I'm afraid. It makes me weak. Reckless. But I don't know how to turn it off.

So I decide I must fight it and the giants at the same time. Reloading once more, I am down to two clips, one short for the number of giants I face.

But I never lose. Never.

Bringing the old Jade back to life, the hard one, the fearless one, I charge, abandoning my cover and taking the giants on out in the open. As the trees disappear behind me, panic gurgles into my chest, but I suffocate it. There is no time for that.

I turn, still running backward, and lift my weapon as a giant runs from the trees, breaking branches on his way out. I fire, aiming at his head as best I can, satisfied when red rains down from the sky moments later. The ground below my feet rumbles when his body falls, and two more appear from the forest before me.

I grab the last clip, prepared for a standoff, but the giants do not wait. They run at me full speed, closing the distance in no time at all. I raise my gun, choosing one at random, firing with every ounce of control I have, keeping the moving target constantly in my aim.

He goes down.

But before I can move, a beefy hand grips my torso, squeezing tight as my arms are crushed against my sides and I am lifted into the air, feet swinging. One move and the giant will slam me into the ground, cracking my skull, ending my short life. I have no time to spare. I need to act. My right hand lands against the hilt of my handgun, and I slide my fingers down into the belt loop, pointer just barely reaching the trigger, but it will do.

I might shoot myself.

I have no other choice.

As I fly up and over the giant's head, I realize the only place left to go is down. I can either fall on my own and risk the injury or slam down with fatal force. Without hesitation, I fire, releasing all six bullets.

One of them grazes my thigh, stinging, drawing blood, but the rest hit their mark, tearing through the nerves of the giant's wrist, and I am free. The grass provides no cushion as I thump against the ground, crunching, yelping in pain. I have no time to think as the giant's other hand reaches for me. I run through his legs as my muscles scream. But there is only one way I can think of to bring a giant down. One weakness I can exploit. I need to remove its height.

Gripping my knife, I slash the thick tendon above the giant's heel. His skin is dense, tough to break through, but my blade cuts true. A pop fills my ear as the tendon gives way and the giant screeches, suddenly unsteady on his feet.

He tries to move, but his foot is no longer useful. He wobbles, confused, and I use the time to snap his other tendon. Unprepared, the giant falls, slamming into the ground. I pull my second handgun free and shoot.

I'm almost sorry as I watch the life leave his eyes. We are all pawns in the queen's game. But a sense of relaxation falls upon the giant's body as his last breath is exhaled, and I wonder if he finally feels free. What must their lives have been like, trapped underneath the castle, far too big for a place so small. Cramped. Broken. Then finally released only to be killed. Did he think he was finally escaping? Did he even know his mind was never his?

Is mine?

"Jade!"

Asher's arms come around me, crushing me into him, and my emotions come flooding back, no longer held off by the fight. My fingers grip his shoulders, holding on for dear life as I ride the torrent. Heat stings my blood, pricks my heart. A heavy weight fills my chest. And I cannot stop the dread from filling my mind.

As my eyes peer over Asher's shoulders, at the curved eyes of the giant lying limp, I cannot help but wonder if I am any different. Have I not been feeling finally free of the queen? Am I fooling myself? Have I walked directly into her plan, falling for the prince, making him trust me, now bringing him to her ripe for the slaughter? In a few days, will it be Asher's empty eyes I stare into?

I dig my hands into his skin, refusing to let go as that dark image invades my sight. Of his indigo eyes, empty, devoid of stars, lifeless.

I won't let it happen.

I can't.

"Are you hurt?" Asher asks, pulling back, searching my eyes.

Pain flares to life in my leg, and I look down as red expands against the fabric of my pants. The bullet took a little more skin than I realized, but nothing that won't heal.

"I'm fine," I say, but my voice does not do a convincing enough job, and before I know it, I find myself swooped into Asher's arms, weightless while he holds me close.

"Asher." I squirm, comfortable in his embrace, but uncomfortable with being rescued.

"Don't worry, you're too heavy to carry all the way to Kardenia," he says, smirking, "There's a medical cabin nearby."

"I can walk."

"Just let me help you," he urges, and because he needs it, I let him. I put my arms around his neck, resting my head against his shoulder, and before I know it, the trip is over.

Asher sets me down gently on a stool inside the small cabin. There is one dirty window bringing light inside, but it is barely enough to see with. Yet Asher seems to know where everything is. A backpack is pulled from the corner, already stuffed full with supplies he gathered in advance. The rebels have been waiting for this day for a while, but I will wait before pestering Asher with questions. We need to be far enough away that he cannot leave me behind. Then I will demand answers. For now, I sit patiently as he grabs extra supplies from the shelves around us.

"Take off your pants," he says while his head is buried in a trunk in the corner.

I flinch as nerves prick my skin. "What?"

"I need to clean your wound," he says, looking back at me, eyebrows raised in question.

"Oh, right," I murmur and stand. But in this small space surrounded by soft light, it feels oddly intimate to remove my clothes. With his back still turned, I sliver out of my jeans, hissing as the fabric scratches my exposed flesh.

"Are you..." He trails off as his eyes wander over my skin. I shiver, but not from the cold. The air feels warm. Static almost. Neither of us moves, but I know when his eyes land on the blood caked against my leg. The mood shifts perceptively and his entire face scrunches tight, as though he's absorbed my pain.

"Sit down," he says, hands holding my shoulders tight to help ease me into a seated position. His fingers gently grace my calf, lifting it onto his bent knee so my entire leg is exposed.

Asher flicks his eyes to me, apologetic, seeking permission and I nod. "This might hurt," he warns before placing a wet cloth to my leg. Rubbing alcohol. I've used it before, scavenged it from the old city. The burn is familiar, but on a wound this large, I bite down, crunching my teeth to keep from screaming out.

The blood rubs away, disappears in the graceful movement of Asher's hands, but my gaze travels north to the determined lock in his jaw, the purse of his lips, the concentration in his eyes. I keep staring, memorizing his face, trying to ignore the pain, stealing his strength as my own.

"I don't think it needs stitches," he tells me as he rubs

a salve into the wound. "It's really not as bad as it looked, just bloody."

I muster the courage to peek back down and see that he's right. My skin is raw for about three inches, but in a narrow stretch, obviously the edge of a bullet. Still, it is a shallow wound and the bleeding has mostly stopped now. In a few days, I will be back to normal, but traveling with it will be more than annoying.

I take the tape as he cleans up the rest of the supplies, and wrap my leg, securing the gauze he used to cover my skin. How many precious resources did Asher just waste on me? Even though they have electricity, I can't imagine medical supplies are easy for the rebels to come by.

"We'll stay here for the night."

Asher pulls a sleeping bag from his backpack, unzipping it.

"I can move, really. Let's go." I want answers, and I won't get them until we leave the rebel camp. I need to know exactly what they're planning, exactly what Asher is planning. I need to know so I can stop him.

Betrayal was unavoidable all along.

Asher hesitates, looking at my leg, looking out the window. He is torn. Time is of the essence, but he does not want to cause me pain. So I take the choice away and stand, gritting my teeth as I pull my jeans back on. Nodding, Asher pulls his backpack together and hands me the other one he's filled.

"This way." He sighs, resigned, as he leads me outside and to the back of the cabin where two bicycles wait, tied up with chains.

My thigh already aches in protest.

Eighteen

We travel for two days before I feel safe enough to start asking questions.

Asher has stopped us in an abandoned house, clean shelter from the rain just starting to drop. Though dusty, the sofa is comfortable below my sore bottom, providing some relief from the pain flaring in my leg. The cut has opened again, so I sit tending the wound while Asher uses the flint to spark the old fireplace back to life.

Our mood has been low for hours, ever since we passed back into the queen's realm. I'm not sure how, but we both felt it when we crossed the dividing line this morning. The air was colder, goose bumps rose along my skin, but underneath I still feel warm, feel like myself. I have no idea how long my self-control will last.

Is it a trick the queen is playing? Or could I have truly broken her curse? I fear I won't know the answer until it is too late.

"Asher?"

He stops adjusting the wood, turning in surprise that I have finally broken the silence after so long. But it's time. Now that we are in the queen's realm, there is no turning back, and I can demand the answers he has been keeping from me, the secrets he is so poorly hiding.

As if he senses what's about to come, Asher leaves the fire, walking slowly back to the couch, sitting down and resting my throbbing leg over his thigh. His fingers run softly over my bare skin, dulling the pain, replacing it with pleasure.

"What do you want to know?"

"Everything."

He won't look at me. I refuse to take my eyes off him. As the silence stretches, I grow impatient, more demanding.

"Start with the plan. Why did the general say you only have one week?"

"Now five days," he mumbles. I wait for him to continue. With a sigh, Asher gives in. "In five days, the general will lead every fighter over the threshold into the queen's realm and they will march on Kardenia, or New York, whatever you want to call it. Before that happens, I need to kill my mother. I need to stop her from trapping more people in her web of magic. The general and I both know that we only have one shot at victory because I'm the only one who can get close enough to the queen to stop her."

"But they don't know the queen is your mother..." I trail off, mind searching for the right words.

"Correct," Asher responds, curt, giving nothing away.

"So why did they give you such an important task? Why do they think you can break through the magic to kill her?"

"Because I told them I could."

"Asher," I bite, tone scathing.

"Fine, fine." He pauses. "When I first arrived at the rebel camp as a boy, no one trusted me. They all thought I was a spy or entranced, under her thrall. And I told them that the queen's magic was weak on children, that they were too innocent to be fully controlled, which was why I was able to run away. That was my first lie, and they believed me."

"Why? Why trust a child? Especially one from a foreign world you don't understand?"

"Because hope makes people trust in lies. They wanted their lost children to be safe, and I gave them a way to believe it could be true."

"What was your second lie?" I ask. Asher looks away. Disgust is evident on his face, self-loathing pulls at his cheeks, strains his neck, wrinkles his lips. I grab his hand, connecting us, trying to let him know it is okay.

"I," Asher says, peeking at me underneath hooded brows, "I told them that once someone breaks the thrall, the queen can never control them again."

I close my eyes tight, shaking my head just slightly. "And that's not true?" My voice is soft, barely a whisper.

"I don't know." His tone is dark, ominous. I know what he is telling me. I understand the second meaning in his words. Asher is confessing what I always knew—I can never be free. The queen can reclaim me at any moment, can pull me back under her thrall. I'm living on borrowed time. Eventually, the frost will freeze my heart, will crystallize my blood.

But right now, my chest is warm, defiant. I'll never go down without a fight.

"I'm so sorry, Jade." Asher's grip tightens on my hand, as his voice grows full. "That's why I didn't want you to come. Why I told you to stay."

"It's okay." I meet his eyes, dark with worry. I know the burden of keeping secrets. I understand the twisted pain, how it snaps the mind in two, pulling the body in opposite directions—what is right and what is necessary. Right now I'm split, torn by my own imminent betrayal, by the secrets I won't reveal. Asher at least is being honest. I wish I could say the same about myself.

Guilty, I look away before he sees the mistruths in my eyes, hoping my skipping heart does not give it away. I decide to change the subject, begin my questioning anew.

"So they sent you to kill her because they believed you're immune. But what will happen when we get there? When the queen uses her powers?"

"I am immune," he admits, "just not for the reasons they think. I'm the heir. I'm one with the magic. It can't affect me."

"Is that why the queen wants you back?"

"Yes and no." Asher's tone has become haggard, as though the words cut when they come out. "I know my mother, and I know when she becomes tired of someone. My father bored her, so she killed him. I disappoint her, so she'll discard me when the time is right."

I've leaned forward, closer to Asher, as though my proximity can protect him. My body is on edge, my nerves prickle in the silence.

"What time is that?"

Asher swallows, eyes absent of their normal sparkle, wet like the ocean at midnight, dark and deep and full of unknowns, rippling with the words he has kept to himself for so long. I want to dive inside, to see him raw, to know every inch of his mind. But I can't. I see only what he gives me, and right now, that's despair.

Asher licks his lips, swallows, and then says the very thing I fear. "When she has another child who can take my place."

Every ounce of fight leaves my body with those words, and I fall back against the couch, defeated, empty.

Asher will die.

He knows it. And now I know it too.

His fate is sealed. The only question is when and

how—by his own hands or the queen's? The answer lies in me.

I stand, overwhelmed, needing an escape from the choice I must make. Do I betray all of the rebels just for the chance that Asher might live? Or do I give in to what he wants and say goodbye forever? Can I?

The queen has no second child. She may never have a second child. But what then? The rebels march, are captured. Asher is locked up, imprisoned in a life he never wanted, only for years to pass unchanging before the queen dies. He will inherit her powers anyway, he will kill himself eventually, and I will end up without him either way. I can lose him now to a fate he chose, or I can lose him after years of bitter hatred have torn us apart.

There is no good option, no choice I want to take.

So I run.

Out the door, abandoning the fire for the cold pellets of rain smacking my skin. Asher calls my name, but I ignore him. The ache in my thigh is comforting in a way, a punishment I deserve for this fate I've given myself. A fate I somehow chose.

The longer I run, the shorter my breath comes, the more strangled, thinner until my lungs feel completely empty. This is how desperation feels. My throat is dry, scratchy, and it burns. My eyes burn too, and I realize the water on my face is not just the rain. It is salty. Bitter. I push myself. When I stop, I'll need to face it, so I won't stop.

Pounding on pavement, my feet sound like thunder. I am the storm. I destroy everything around me.

"Jade!"

Asher's voice melts me, pulls me toward him like a magnet, and I stumble. Bent at the waist, I heave, quickly trying to fill a chest that has stopped working. I cough. And when that does not work, I give in to the burn. Through the patter of rain, my sobs sound animalistic, howls that hang in the air around me, echoing in my ears.

I don't even know what I'm crying for.

Asher?

My mother?

Maddy?

The rebels?

Myself?

Too many images flood my mind, too many choices, too many lives that hang in the balance.

"Shh." Asher tries to soothe as his arms encircle me, try to comfort me. "Shh, it'll be okay."

But it won't. And I'm furious.

My blood boils as I turn in his arms. Just as quickly as my tears came, they are gone, replaced by a crimson tide I cannot control. So I ride it, throwing myself out of Asher's embrace, pushing against his chest so we stumble apart.

"Why?" My voice is manic. The rain begins to fall thicker, creating a wall between our bodies, gray and foggy, just clear enough to see through.

Asher is confused, uncertain. He remains silent, eyes never leaving me, lips curling into his mouth. His fingers rise, stretching for my arm, trying to close the distance, but I swat him away.

"Why, Asher? Why did you do this to me? If you knew this was how it would end the entire time, why did you make me feel? Why—" But I cut myself off. I won't say it. I refuse.

"I don't know," he says, stepping back.

"That's not good enough," I shout, closing in, shoving my hands into his hard chest, pushing him back once more. "There are a thousand people in the guard, why did you have to take me?"

I pound his chest again. He stumbles back. I hit him harder, determined to beat the words out of him. I know it's not fair. I know it's not all his fault, that I carry blame too. But I'm too far gone to care. And when he still doesn't talk, I throw my fists at him once more. This time, Asher catches my wrists tight, yanking me toward him so I fall against his chest.

"Because I'm selfish," he tells me, tone even. I squirm, trying to break free, but he won't let go. He tugs me closer.

"You are," I spit, because words are my only weapon now. They do not faze him. He does not even flinch.

"As soon as I saw you, I wanted to know more. Needed to. Maybe it was how quickly you snatched my gun, or the fire in your eyes, or the fact that you let me go. I don't know. I was taken. I couldn't think about anything else." Asher's tone has grown frenzied. His eyes dart around my face, looking everywhere but my eyes, as though he is trying to memorize every curve, every spot.

And then the pace slows, his expression grows tender, calm. His gaze drifts from my lips to my nose, higher until it meets mine. "You were so beautiful, but so hard, so cold. When I looked at you, I saw caged fire. Your spark was almost gone. It was smothered, slowly dying. And all I wanted to do was set you free."

He releases my wrists, doing just that, but I don't move. I can't. My feet are stuck to the ground. My muscles have grown tight in the rain.

Would I rather be safely back on the wall, oblivious to the way passion burns the skin, ignorant of the heat it pulses through my veins? Or would I rather be here, torn between two impossible choices, but aflame with feeling?

That answer is easy.

I lift my hand to his wet cheek. We only have five days left, and I do not want to waste them with more words. I want to fill them with a lifetime of memories, brilliant constellations to guide me through the dark, because a starless night is fast approaching.

In this moment, my decision has become clear.

I'm not strong enough to let him go. Not strong enough to let him die. To just give in. I'm a fighter. I don't know how to do anything else. And I refuse to believe there are no other options, that there is no way to save him. But when I betray him, I fear Asher will never look at me this way again, like my eyes hold every wish he's ever dreamed.

Soon he will hate me.

But right now, there is only him and me. Alone in the rain. Inches apart. Breath mingling. Proclamations unspoken but there all the same.

I don't know who moves first, I just know that we are touching, kissing, grasping for one another. I give in, lost in the feel of his skin on mine. I let go, falling so fast that even Asher cannot catch me.

Nineteen

It's amazing how quickly time slips through your fingers. Blink and it's gone. I never understood how fleeting it was until right now, staring across the dried up bed of the Hudson River, at the broken skyline I would recognize anywhere, at the castle that haunts my thoughts.

Asher and I have spent four days pedaling as fast as we could, four nights touching as slow as we could, and now there is nothing left. The rebels march tomorrow, which means Queen Deirdre must die today.

But she won't.

And that single thought stabs my chest, an open wound.

Asher tried to say goodbye last night, but I could not bear to hear the words. Every syllable was a knife to my heart, pain I deserve to feel for what I am about to do. As we lay under the stars in each other's arms, he held me close, catching my tears with his lips. In that moment, I almost broke. Almost confessed. But that would accomplish nothing, would not save him. So I held him close, hugged my face into his chest so my lips could not open, could not speak.

We stayed that way, silent, not even kissing, just embracing until the sun rose. I've never hated dawn before, but this morning it was my enemy, unrelenting and impossible to defeat.

Asher takes my lifeless hand, squeezing it gently, trying to let me know that it will all be okay. I tighten my grip, wondering if he has guessed why my throat holds no words, why the days have passed with so little conversation. Does he know it is because every time I open my mouth to speak, I fear what I might say? That even a glance might give my betrayal away?

But there is no need to worry. Trust shines like a vibrant flame in his eyes, one that will soon be snuffed out.

I break his hold, unable to bear the sincerity in his gaze, and mount my bike, pedaling ahead of him. Asher follows quickly behind me and we dip through the entrance of the Lincoln Tunnel, to the spot where it all began.

The rickety squeak of wheels sounds slightly foreboding to my ears, and as we descend underground with only candlelight to guide us, I realize how much I miss my horse. There's something silly about riding into battle on a bike. My guns are reloaded and strapped to my hips, bulky. My sword bounces against my leg. Even my crossbow slides down my shoulder so I must constantly shrug to keep it in place.

I am awkward, graceless. My butt hurts. I miss the feel of muscles coiling and extending beneath my legs, empowering and strong. The sound of thunderous steps, galloping at full speed, making my heart race with excitement. But even my horse could not bring a thrill to my veins, not today.

All too soon, sunlight reappears as a speck in the distance, enlarging until we have reached the end. We leave our bikes to climb over the heap of fallen rocks blocking the exit, maneuvering through the rubble as I lead him around the location of the mines.

Before we know it, Asher and I are back in New York. Neither of us says anything as we pass the pharmacy where we first met, first fought. I'm too distracted. I don't want to think about the first time Asher decided to trust me, when he saved my life because he thought he saw something brave in my eyes. But I'm a coward, and I'm waiting for him to realize it too.

Wordlessly, we walk. Both lost in our own thoughts. But our fingers squeeze together tightly, bound together, giving me strength.

Asher and I have gone over this plan countless times during the past few days. I'm to present him to the queen as my prisoner, and when we get close to her, he will make his move. That, at least, is what he believes. So when we reach the very edge of Central Park, just beyond sight of the wall, he does not protest as I pull his arms behind his back and secure them loosely with a rope.

Three knives are hidden under the cotton shirt covering his torso. A gun is strapped around his thigh, reachable through the hole in his pant leg pocket. He does not realize that I took the bullets out in the middle of the night. He never thought to double check.

In this instant, we are no longer a boy and girl. From now on, I am a Black Heart and Asher is my prisoner. We will play our parts until we're delivered to the queen. No speaking. No lingering glances. No tender touching. Though he believes it is just an act, I know differently. I understand that this is the way it was always going to end. In hatred. In betrayal.

Happy just doesn't have a place in my story.

I take a deep, uneven breath, and push Asher forward, steeling myself, prepared to begin. But he stills me with one word.

"Jade."

My heart stops.

He knows.

But when he looks over his shoulder, promises blaze in his eyes. Fire and warmth fill his irises, and I know exactly what is coming next. The goodbye I would not let him say. The words that would be too painful to hear.

Asher's mouth dips open.

"Stop," I croak, voice broken like the city that raised me. "I can't take it."

Asher's brows furrow, hurt, but he nods like he understands. And I want to shake him, no you don't know, but my hands do not move. He is too gentle. Too trusting. Maybe I would be too if things were different. If life wasn't so cruel.

But it is.

And my fragile heart cannot take anymore. If I hear those words dancing in his gaze, I might give in. I might give up and let Asher have his way.

But I can't. I won't lose him to death. I would rather he hate me.

So I look away, breaking the moment, and Asher steps forward letting me know that it is okay, that it is hard for him too, that he's ready.

It takes fifteen minutes for us to reach the wall.

My hands tremble, my palms sweat, my heart races. But on the outside my expression is calm, my face is blank. I know when my old comrades spot me because a black speck on the wall jumps into motion. Even from a distance I see him run to the nearest guard tower.

My pace does not slow or quicken. I steel my nerves, encircle my body in a hard shell that no one will be able to crack. I become my namesake. I am not cold or cursed. The queen's magic does not fill me. I am trapped in a spell that is entirely my doing. But it is the only way I know to carry on.

The gate to the city opens when we are just a few feet away. Inside, hands behind his back and feet shoulder width apart, the commander waits.

I search his eyes for a speck of relief, a dot of warmth, any morsel that lets me know some worry has been eased by my safe return. But they are blank, just as emotionless as I remember. I wait for disappointment to tighten my chest, but nothing comes because really, this is exactly what I expected.

"Jade," his deep voice closes the space between us.

"Commander Alburn." I nod in greeting, a subordinate to her leader, not a daughter to her father. "I have brought the queen her son."

Asher plays his part well, refusing to meet the commander's eyes, struggling against my grip as I mention his mother. I hold him steady, jerking his shoulders straight, rough in my movements.

"You are not in uniform." The commander upturns his nose in distaste, inspecting both Asher and me, pausing on my black heart pin with a slight nod. "But the queen will want to see you immediately."

He shouts commands that are followed without protest, and a carriage is brought before us. I shove Asher in first, distracted by the stares of the guard, not paying attention, and his forehead bangs against the door. My face remains serene as he groans in pain. My arms do not flinch as I force him into a seat and make my way inside. But guilt invades my system. Then I remember that this pain is nothing compared to what I am about to inflict. Nausea rots my stomach, and I swallow, but the unease will not go away.

"Where have you been these past weeks?" The commander asks, closing the door. Not a moment later, the carriage rolls into motion, bumpy over these ill paved streets.

He knew the queen's plan, so I am not sure why he bothers asking the question. There is a wary gleam in his eye that concerns me, as though he knows the queen no longer controls me. The tiny cabin suddenly feels too small. I cannot look at the commander. I cannot look at Asher. So I turn my face to the window, watching stone homes pass by, but even the old buildings seem to judge me.

"I was captured by the rebels and brought back to their base where I remained imprisoned until little over a week ago. I recognized the prince and did not want to free myself until I could also detain him and return him to Queen Deirdre. A few days ago, the camp was attacked and I was finally able to act. I returned as quickly as I was able."

"I see," he draws the last word out. "The queen and I were concerned that you had perhaps lost your way."

My palms are beginning to sweat. Does the queen know I am no longer loyal? Her frosty curse does not invade my insides. In fact, warmth seeps into my skin, making me hot, confined, about to faint.

The cart shifts angles and through the window, the town begins to shrink. We have started the ascent to the castle, up the winding mountainside, and I'm reminded that it does not matter. By her magic or mine, the queen will get her way. Asher will be caught and that is all that matters to her.

"She has plans for you Jade, plans I cannot reveal but which require your dedication."

I rein my emotions in, force my breath to calm.

"I have never failed before, Commander." I turn from the window, pulling my eyes away from the rising height, meeting his cold stare with one of my own. Empty. Hard. Focused. My voice has migrated back to its old flatness as I tell him the truth. "I do not intend to start now."

A grim smile and nod is my only response.

Asher's eyes flick to me, an aura in my peripheral, concerned. He cannot tell if it is still an act or if the queen is starting to pull me under the thrall. I wonder if he is starting to catch on, if he could even fathom that this is entirely my doing. I'm not sure I want to know. I stay straight, face forward, detached.

A drowsy chill has settled over my system, dull but still there, haunting almost. A sense of calm trickles down my limbs, stilling the nervousness. Part of me feels completely ready for what is about to occur. Part of me wants to scream. I grasp onto the second part, keeping that fire close to my heart, burning. I have not betrayed him yet, so I hold on to these last few minutes of passion. Warmth permeates the space between my body and Asher's, pushing and pulling so I cannot shirk the awareness of his skin so close to mine. We do not touch, even the barest brush of fingers might give me away, but the heat is enough.

I hold on to it.

I want to remember what it felt like when he loved me.

The carriage pulls to a stop and the fire dissolves.

An odd sense of déjà vu settles over my system as we exit, almost in slow motion. Nothing feels real. I'm somewhere else, watching like a spectator as this imposter prepares to destroy the one man she's ever loved, the person who saved her.

It was not so long ago that I came here to meet the queen, that I received my mission. Yet the world is changed. The wrought iron gates are less majestic, the tall spires less intimidating now that I have seen and killed the creatures that built them. Even the sky has adopted a hazy gray color, clouding over and eliminating the stark blue, no longer reminiscent of the queen's eyes. Now they mirror my stormy mood.

We approach, climbing the steps to the front door. Asher's feet are sluggish, and I must press against his back to keep him moving. His head swivels, glancing everywhere. His pulse quickens beneath my fingers, a fine sheen of sweat glistens on the back of his neck. Asher's movements become frenetic, ticking this way and that. Afraid or apprehensive, I don't know.

I do know that I am oddly empty. Spent. With each step, my heart grows harder, colder. I am bracing myself for what is to come.

As we make our way down the dark hallway, the cavernous throne room slowly comes into view. I wonder what waits. Will soldiers jump on us the moment we pass by, securing both of our arms, locking us away? Or did the queen always know that in the end I would not fail her?

The commander stops.

I push Asher past him, stepping into the brightly lit room.

The queen smiles from her throne. Crimson robes drape elegantly down the front of the wooden dais, flowing like a pool of blood around her. Lit from above by hidden windows, the golden crown blazes like fire, casting metallic reflections on her blonde hair, making it seem jeweled. Power exudes across the space between us—power and confidence.

No guards line the walls. No soldiers. No protectors.

We are alone.

Why then, am I more afraid than ever?

Twenty

"Your Majesty." I bow as deeply as I can given that my hands still hold Asher's binds. He is struggling against me, but it doesn't quite feel real. If he wanted to, Asher could break my grip easily, even with his hands tied. His strength greatly exceeds my own. Which means he still trusts me. Still believes in me, even as I deviate from the plan we discussed for hours on end.

Our skin brushes together while he moves, little kisses that ignite the nerves in my hands. The flares are distracting, if only because I know I will never feel them again. My resolve is firm, but I'm not sure how much longer I will last. Fear clutches my heart. Trepidation stalls my movements.

Before I can give into the doubts, I act.

Shoving as hard as I can, I push Asher forward. He tumbles across the floor, unprepared, bashing his head against the tile since his hands are not free to catch him.

When his body comes to rest, his face turns, finds me. A bloody cut has opened, dripping down the pristine skin of his forehead, covering the eyes I love so much. But it doesn't hide the confusion spreading across his features.

Asher still doesn't understand.

"I have brought you your son." I almost wince at the sound of my voice. Was it always this sharp? This cruel?

As though the words have hit him like a physical force, a tremor shutters down Asher's body, curls it in tighter so he looks almost like a little boy. "Jade?" he whispers, soft.

I don't meet his eyes. I'm too afraid of what I'll find. Though my body is still, my mind screams that there is time to stop, to help Asher, to heed his wishes.

But what about my wish? I want to see him live.

I will see him live.

"Please don't do this," he pleads, words meant only for my ears. And the lullaby in his voice lulls me, pulls me in, as though entranced. I want to remain impassive, a stone statue, but I cannot. My eyes travel slowly down, across the floor, to where he lays, a heap on the floor.

The moment our eyes meet, I know what I must do.

All this time, I was given every opportunity to tell Asher the truth, to confess that he never really captured me, that it was all part of a greater plan. But I never did. Why? I did not want to hurt him, not when we had begun to grow close. There was never a good time, no opportune moment.

In the end, I couldn't bear to lose him—at least that is what I told myself. But now I wonder if it was something else?

What if deep down, I always knew that I would need this last weapon, one great lie that will convince the queen I belong to her, will convince Asher I never belonged to him? I keep my gaze locked on his as I open my mouth and say the words I never could before.

"I have followed my orders, Your Majesty. As asked, I allowed your son to capture me and bring me to the rebel camp. I convinced him to trust me and now have returned him to you unharmed."

Understanding dawns. The changes to Asher's features are small at first, the curl of his lip, the furrow of his brow, the flare of his nostrils. His angles slowly grow harsh, turn accusing. The darkness spreads, stealing the light from his indigo eyes, snuffing out the stars I love so much, the ones that seemed to guide me home. Now we are both lost, adrift at sea, anchorless and without direction.

Deep in his irises, I see the truth. Though anger flares across his skin, down in the depths of his soul all that exists is pain. His heart has cracked, small at first, but spreading, extending, shattering slowly enough that he experiences each fracture. I know, because my chest feels the same, so hot with hurt that I cannot move, can barely breathe.

I find the will to pull my gaze away, snapping any connection we ever had, and my heart finally bursts to pieces.

The queen watches me with interest, a small smile across her lips. I am dead inside. Rotted to my core, so ashamed that I might crumble at any second, broken down from the inside out. But that only makes my act stronger. My features are stony, hard. I do not cry. I am barely aware of the world around me.

The queen stands, stepping down off her throne. Each click of her shoes echoes across the small room, and I hold myself steady. Asher's eyes burn my cheeks, a weapon as his glare digs under my skin. But we've come too far to stop now.

"Very well done," the queen says as she approaches. I wait for her magic to call on me, to freeze my insides. But I am not five years old anymore. I have lived. I have made choices that will haunt the rest of my years. And as her icy fingers brush my cheeks, cool and cold, I realize she cannot touch me.

My heart is already gone. Tattered. Shredded and broken on the floor beside my feet. There is nothing in my soul for her to take because I have destroyed it already. The frost does not cover my insides, does not burn my memories away. They are all too real, too raw. The queen cannot bury me in her snowflakes. Her crystals do not crawl their way through my veins.

Our eyes meet and in that moment our thoughts are the same, I am finally free, just as she promised. But at what price?

"Jade." She sighs, but it is a sound filled with warmth, with excitement. Her fingers continue to caress my cheek, but the touch has become loving in a way, motherly. "I am so proud of the work you've done. You have no idea. I sent you out into the world a little girl, and you have returned more of a woman than I dared hope."

"Stop," Asher growls. My heart clenches tight. I have never heard his voice sound so ugly. "Just stop."

He stands and the rope falls to the floor behind him. Asher has untied my knots, but he does not reach for the knives at his waist. He does not reach for the gun strapped to his thigh. He reaches for me.

I am immobile as his soft hand grabs my arm, pulling me away from the queen, pulling me toward him. I cannot breathe as heat floods my veins. Pain or pleasure, I'm not sure. His fingers travel up until his palms hold my face tight, force my eyes to meet his, demanding, still unable to believe what he is seeing.

"I know what you're doing, Jade, and I won't let you." His fingers grip tighter, and I realize that Asher has guessed the truth—he has read it in my eyes. He knows that I will not let him die. Even in the face of my betrayal, he has chosen to see the good in me.

I don't deserve such loyalty.

It takes all my strength to keep my hands at my side, to not throw them around his neck, to stay away. I imagine his lifeless corpse dead on the ground. The vision pushes me through, helps me carry on, because in the end this will all be worth it.

Asher will be alive.

And I will endure any pain to make sure that happens.

"I don't know what you mean." My voice is even, steady.

"Don't do this to us."

"There is no us. I'm not who you think I am. I never was."

"I know exactly who you are, Jade. I knew it the day I met you and I know it now. You're the only one who's ever been confused," he whispers, sad, wiping my cheek one more time, as though catching an invisible tear. But I don't miss the movement of his other hand as it slips beneath his shirt, searching for a knife.

So that is how this will end. The same way it began.

A fight.

I have no choice but to stop him. I need the queen to believe me, to trust that I am loyal to her unconditionally. Somehow, I know the answer is there. The way to save Asher's life rests deep in the secrets of Queen Deirdre's black heart. I'm sure of it. Why else would she need him returned unharmed? Why else did she ask me to retrieve him? We are just pawns in her plan. But if it means saving his life, I will gladly play my part.

Asher pulls a silver blade free and I attack.

He anticipates my punch and sidesteps it easily. But I

find my footing and surge forward, aiming a kick at his abdomen. I connect. He grunts, dropping the knife, wheeling around to turn his focus completely on me.

The queen plays bystander, watching as though we are actors in a play, amused. The commander moves to intervene as Asher and I circle one another, but she waves him off.

This is our battle. Our fight.

I run forward, tired of the delay, but Asher takes my hands, flipping me over his back so I land hard on the ground, wind knocked out of my lungs. I cough, finding my breath, and stand again.

But before I even reach my knees, he punches me in the stomach and I roll, world flipping upside down then right side up again. I meet his eyes and find despair. I have forced him into this. I have pushed my gentle prince aside, have broken his spirit, have turned him into someone he does not recognize.

Asher grabs my arms and throws me to the side. I do not even try to fight back. Because I know who he is, and I know that in the end he won't be able to do it.

I watch as he dips his hand into his pocket, retrieving the handgun we hid there. The black metal is unnatural against his ivory skin, evil in the hands of a person who is so good. A tear falls free from Asher's eye as he raises the weapon higher, points the barrel at his mother's heart.

I wonder if he feels that it is lighter than it should be,

or if that sort of knowledge is only reserved for people like me, people who consider deadly weapons an extra appendage, as easy to use as my hands or feet.

My eyes drift to the queen. No panic shines in her eyes, no doubt. Like me, she knows who her son is. She knows she has nothing at all to fear.

The click of the safety being removed is deafening to my ear. Asher tightens his shaking hand, grasping the hilt with fingers firm, determined, resolute.

Time halts.

I want to scream at Asher, tell him not to do it, that he will hate himself. If he shoots, even though no bullet will fly out, the boy I love will break. Will disappear. But I can't say anything. All I can do is trust that he is not the murderer he is trying to be.

His finger dips down to the trigger.

And then nothing. He holds it there. Body shaking.

He cannot shoot.

Asher throws the gun to the side and falls to his knees, releasing a scream that rips his insides raw, tears its way out of his throat. The mourning of a man who faced his destiny and could not see it through.

But on the inside, I smile with relief. I don't know what Asher's destiny is, but I know it was not that. He was never meant to be a killer.

I walk over slowly, confident that all the fight has left him, and bind Asher's hands once more. He does not stir.

Does not move. I want to weep for him, but I cannot. I want to brush away his tears, but I pull my hands back to my side.

"Commander Alburn, take my son away," the queen drawls, distaste evident in her voice. I wonder for a moment if she wanted him to shoot, just to prove her wrong.

Instead she takes my hand. "Come, Jade."

I yearn to turn my head, to look at Asher one more time. Even if his eyes shine with hatred, I want to see them. I want a last look that I can hold close. But I have come too far to turn back now. Though Asher is alive, he must be dead to me. That is the price I paid to save his life. So I step emotionless with the queen. My heart is worn out. My mind can hardly think. Even though I am victorious, I am empty inside.

She leads me to the balcony where this all began, where she gave me my assignment, and in my naïveté I said yes.

"You have proven yourself to me today, Jade. It takes a very special person to break my curse. No one has done it before, but I hoped you would."

"Why?" I ask, emboldened.

"Do you know how the magic works?"

"Asher told me," I whisper. "He said he was the heir, that the magic would pass to him after you died."

I look away, afraid that the pain in my eyes will reveal the truth. My gaze drops down to my home. The stone houses. The wall. The corroding metal. Beyond to the ocean, to the point where it meets the sky, extending farther and farther, until earth and air become one. How stupid I was to think I would ever be free of this place. To see possibilities on the horizon.

"Yes, he would. But my son never cared much for the magic, never wanted to learn the lessons I tried to teach him. And in doing so, sealed his own fate."

My head snaps up. "You're not going to kill him, are you?"

I try to control my voice, to seem impassive. But she is not watching me. Her eyes are on the sky.

"No, I'm going to replace him." She pauses, looks down at me, and I know everything is about to change. The queen is going to tell me her secrets. My heart grows lighter and I stifle a smile, because in her words I know I'll find the key to Asher's life, his freedom. All of the pain pricking my chest will be worth it.

"My son is weak. He is too merciful to rule, and though I tried for many years, no second child has ever filled my womb. And then our worlds merged, and I met a little girl who was unafraid, fearless, and I thought perhaps my luck had changed. So I let the commander raise you, teach you to fight. You grew strong, willful. You learned to take what you wanted because the world would not hand it to you. And all the while I watched from a distance. But now you are ready."

I can't breathe.

Can't think.

Here it comes. Asher's only hope. My soul's salvation.

The queen grasps my hands, but I don't feel her skin. I am aware of nothing but the words waiting on her lips.

"Blood is not the only thing that can define an heir. As with all things magic, there are loopholes. But the rules are very precise, and only someone strong enough to break my spell can become my new heir... Someone like you."

A bomb explodes in my head. But the debris is not chaotic, it is organized, it falls like puzzle pieces, finding one another, forming a picture that grows ever clearer.

I am going to be Queen Deirdre's new heir.

When she dies the magic will fall on me.

I stumble, holding onto the railing, bringing a smile to my face as though I am excited, but in truth my insides scream. The queen puts her arm around my shoulders, as affectionate as I've ever seen her. I am too numb to pull away.

How did I not see this before?

Now that the truth has been laid bare before me, it is so obvious. For a mere moment in time, I allowed myself to believe Asher and I would be together, that somehow we would save each other, that in the end our love would defy the odds. I let myself hope. But it blinded me to the one certainty I should have known all along.

Our story has always been a tragedy.

Asher and I were destined to meet, but not because of love. He was born into the wrong role. Asher is the good one, the gentle soul, the hero. And the fates needed to correct their mistake, so they led him to me.

The soldier. The killer.

I am the one destined to put a bullet in Queen Deirdre's head.

I am the one destined to die.

Twenty-One

I thought betraying Asher was the worst thing I would ever do. I was wrong.

The rebels march on Kardenia, and like lambs to the slaughter, I will lead them to their doom. For over a week the queen has been tracking their movement with her power, and last night they set up camp just outside New York. Now I am marching beyond the wall, on my way to greet them, to tell them the queen is dead. Then I will lure them into Kardenia, making their worst nightmare come true.

I'm not sure why the queen does not pull them into her thrall already, why she didn't do it days ago, why I have been sent to retrieve them, to betray them as well.

Is it another test of my loyalty?

Is her magic not as strong as I believe?

Or does she simply get pleasure from witnessing other people's pain?

Either way, I have no choice. Queen Deirdre has not mentioned the heir transferal again. I have no idea how it works, what I must do, if Asher is even involved. And until that magic washes over me, until I am confident that I have the tools necessary to destroy her, I will do exactly as she says.

Ahead, the end of the tree line filters into view, the divider between the forest of Central Park and the metal wreckage of old New York. Over my shoulder, the castle looms above the edge of the wall, overlooking the city, as visible in the skyline as any skyscraper. A white flag billows atop the highest spire, flopping in the sun, brilliantly catching the light. It was to be Asher and my signal that all was clear, that the queen was dead and the rebels could approach the city. But now it is an omen of the frost about to invade their bodies, the crystalline ivory that will soon incase their hearts. A sense of dread fills my veins, slowing me as though a physical weight has been pressed against my chest.

I will free them.

That is the only thought carrying me through. Just like I will save Asher, I will save everyone that I curse this day. A little bit of time and two bullets are all I need. Then everyone in this city will be free, forever.

I take a deep breath, using those promises to calm myself, to prepare for the lies about to come. Closing my eyes tight, I turn back around. In the black haven behind my lids, my heartbeat slows, my mind clears, the catch in my throat disappears. I swallow and then open my eyes, ready.

I know the rebels are out here somewhere, hidden within my metal city. My gaze travels over the broken lines before me—the bent iron, the shattered glass, the crumbling stone—searching for human life. These ruins have been my playground for years. It's only a matter of time before I find them.

The search begins on Eighth Avenue, the route I told General Willis he should take when approaching Kardenia. The streets are clean, the road leads easily to the wall, and it is wide enough to hold an army.

I barely walk ten blocks before I see them approaching, decorated in all different clothes—ashen grays, deep blacks, camouflaged greens. There is no reason, no uniform, but I like it. Somehow it seems the exact way freedom fighters should look. They do not stop when they see me, but instead press forward until we are only a few feet apart. I don't fail to notice that they have not lowered their weapons.

I raise my empty hands, open, trying to convey that I come as a friend, I come in victory, and there is no reason to fight. Though my muscles are tight, anxious about what I must do, a smile comes easily to my face. Despite it all, I am happy to see these people. Excited even. The rebel base had started to feel like home, and I miss it.

From behind the front line, General Willis steps

through the crowd. The silver in his hair catches the light and his face is grooved with shadows. Out in the open, drenched in sunlight, he looks smaller than I remembered. Frailer. Older.

"Where is Asher?" he asks. No greeting. No hello. Though I try not to care, it stings, a little puncture in my chest.

I swallow the hurt back down. "He waits for us in the city." Not a lie, not quite. But those will come eventually.

"Our electronics stopped working a few days ago. Why?"

Internally, I shake my head. The rebels should have stopped. They should have known not to march for that exact reason, but they had hope. Hope in Asher. Hope in me. Hope that they would see their families once again. The second they crossed into the queen's realm, their fate was sealed. Even if I fail today, even if they kill me, I have no doubt that she will enthrall them, control them, bring them into the folds of her city.

That is the exact reason I must press on.

"There is something Asher did not tell you," my voice is airy, too quiet to be convincing. I force conviction into the words even as I hate myself for using Asher's deepest secret against him. Stronger, fuller, I continue. "He is the queen's son. He was always immune to her power because he was her heir. And when we killed her, those powers transferred to him. The magic is not gone, not yet."

"He tricked us," the general curses. Weapons click all around me, the subtle shift that means they are ready to fire. My heart sinks just a little. Asher and I were never one of these people, not really. We've only ever had each other.

"No." My voice is sad, hurt. I am not acting at all. "He never meant to hurt you. Asher is going to take his own life. He is going to sacrifice himself. He just wanted to say goodbye first."

I'm not sure if the general is convinced. He makes no move against me. He makes no move at all. Jaw locked, eyes narrowed, he tries to read me. Doubt blazes in his eyes. But the row of guns behind him wobbles. They all want so badly to believe me, to believe that a decade of fighting is finally going to end in victory.

"Do you really think we would be standing here talking if Asher wanted to keep the magic, to reign like his mother?" Disgust burns my throat, sharpens my tone, adds a bite. How can they really think Asher would betray them? After everything he wanted to give up, his own life. Indignation boils my blood. How dare they doubt him. Now more than ever, I'm glad I stopped him, my gentle prince. These people never deserved his sacrifice.

"If Asher wanted to use the magic, you would all be cursed right now, faster than you could blink. But you're not. And inside that city, everything you've ever wanted since the earthquake waits for you." My chiding is working, perhaps because real anger fuels my words, or perhaps because of their own guilt. I'm not sure. But I do know the weapons are starting to lower, that even General Willis is growing soft.

"Please," I add. My voice cracks, breaks. I am no longer thinking of Asher, I am thinking of myself. Of what I will give up to save them. Of what I've already given up. And all of it will be for nothing if I can't convince the rebels to continue on, if I can't convince the queen that I am capable of endless betrayal, that I am just like her.

"Please, don't let him die for nothing. All he wants is to save you all. Please, go into the city, find your loved ones, and make his dying wish come true." Though I say him, I mean me. I don't want to die for nothing. I want to save them all. It is my dying wish that I will see come true.

Sincerity pulses through my words, a force that washes over the rebels, relaxes them. A buzz begins to stir the air, almost palpable, a tingle of excitement. One man folds, stepping out of formation. Hope shines through the tears wetting his eyes.

"Please," I whisper, voice thick with words unspoken. Please forgive me. That is what I want to say, what I can't say.

But they hear something else. *Please believe me.*

The dam breaks.

All around me, men and women abandon their stations, first walking and then running down the street, air whipping my face as they pass by. Stuck immobile in the middle of the human river flowing around me, I remember Asher's words from a few nights before.

Hope can be a beautiful thing. It can guide you through the dark. It can make you feel safe even in the most dangerous of times. But in the wrong hands, in my hands, hope is a weapon, bait to dangle before believing eyes.

I follow slowly after the crowd, no interest in seeing the fire disappear from their eyes. It is only a matter of time before they reach the city, before they realize their families are not free, before the queen pulls them under her control. I meander over concrete, lost in my own thoughts, barely aware when I pass back into the greenery of the park, not paying attention as the wall slips into view.

"Jade," a voice calls.

I turn, surprised. By now I thought the queen's curse would have taken hold, that the rebels would be no more. But a single figure leans like a shadow against a tree, hidden beneath leaves, just shy of stepping into view.

My heart sinks.

I would recognize that voice anywhere, the excitement laced tone, the frenetic nature.

"Maddy," I say, slowly, as though I can't quite believe my eyes.

Before I can move, Maddy jumps into the light, throwing her arms around me, locking me into an enthusiastic hug. My arms hang limp by my side, useless. My body has gone numb, dead.

"What are you doing here?" I whisper. Could the queen have possibly planned this? Have seen it coming? Must I lie to everyone who has ever shown me kindness?

"I was so worried about you and Asher. I mean, totally confident, but still, worried." She leans back, grinning and staring at me, before pulling me back down into a firm embrace. Her fingers clutch too tightly, her arms hold on for a second too long, and I realize there is more than just excitement behind her words. There is fear as well, laced into her voice, bringing her pitch a note too high.

I raise my arms, bringing them around her, trying to ease her fears. Soon she won't be able to feel them anyway. Soon all of that worry will be gone. But so will everything else.

"What's wrong? Why haven't you joined the others inside?"

We separate and Maddy crosses her arms, shrugs, bites her lip. Anxious fingers tap on her bicep and her cheeks twitch with indecision. When I first met Maddy, human contact made me uncomfortable. It was foreign. Unfamiliar. But since then so much has changed, and it is completely natural to reach out, covering her hand with mine, calming her nervous movements.

Our eyes meet.

"I'm just," she starts, pauses, takes a deep breath. "What if he's not...not there? You know? What if he's really gone?"

Maddy doesn't have to say anything else. I know exactly whom she means. Her father. My mouth goes dry. I have no idea what to say, how to ease her pain.

"I know it's stupid, I mean I haven't even seen him in ten years, if he is dead nothing will change, it'll be just like it's been. But—"

Her eyes start to water. In those shimmering pools, I see my reflection and cringe. Soon Maddy will forget her father. He will fade into memory, trapped inside her ice-cold heart, lost. And in the split second before that happens she will know that I am the one who broke her dreams, who stole them away, who in essence killed her father. In her wavering voice, I hear the cries of a thousand people, all cursing my name, all broken by my betrayal.

"But what if he is there?" I finish her sentence. Maddy nods, unable to say the words herself. "There's only one way to find out."

I grab her hand, entwining our fingers, trying to give her all my strength. It works. Her eyes lose their wrinkles and her brows pull apart, no longer scrunched together in a tight knot.

As we walk toward the open front gate of the wall, part of me actually thinks we might find him before the queen lays down her curse, that Maddy will be reunited with him first, that maybe I can do one good thing amidst so much treachery. Maybe then she won't hate me so much when she wakes up and remembers what I've done.

Inside, the streets are crowded. The rebels fill the winding roads, weapons forgotten and replaced with old, broken down photographs. Names are being shouted loudly, over and over, intermixing so it sounds like a jumble of noise. I cannot pull the words apart. But it does not matter because the citizens of Kardenia have not been moved to action. They do not leave their homes. Even if they hear their names, I doubt they will understand what it means, who is shouting for them.

Maddy's hand tightens on mine. Her nails dig into my palms.

For a moment, I think she's spotted her father, somehow, somewhere, a face pressed against the glass or a head poking through a window in curiosity.

"I…"

My insides knot in understanding as she trails off. Still connected through our fingers, I halt, turning to meet her suddenly confused gaze.

"Jade, I feel cold."

Maddy drops my hand as her eyes blank, lose focus. The beautifully dark skin on her face grows ashen, depleted of the energy that once filled it. Her lips open to speak, but then close, empty. As the moments pass, she continues to grow unrecognizable.

All around me, the mood shifts. The streets grow quiet, still. Hands drop lifeless to people's sides. Some even sit down on the floor, unable to remain standing. I have never seen the queen's magic in action before. I have lived with the cursed for my whole life, surrounded by it, but that was different. We were all already under the thrall. I've never watched the magic take hold. Observing it now, traces of fear and sadness trickle into my system. The city has gone comatose.

I understand why the queen waited so long. She wanted me to appreciate what I am to inherit, wanted to gift me with a display of the power I will one day hold. She finally believes she has an heir who will see the magic the way she sees it, as beautiful, wondrous, intoxicating.

But all I see is the monster I will someday become.

Silence spreads through the city as the rebels fall one by one, almost in slumber, bodies motionless on the ground except for the rise and fall of breathing chests.

Movement catches my peripheral vision as cheers filter into my ears. The Black Hearts are descending from their hiding spots on the wall, victorious over the rebels they have sought long and hard to defeat.

I want to scream. A burning ache fills my chest, scratches my throat, singes my eyes.

They don't even know. They have no idea who they've just ensnared, that those are not just bodies on the ground. Those are their mothers and fathers, their brothers and sisters. Those are the people who wanted to save us all from ourselves, from the queen. If they knew, they would not clap. They would weep instead.

I kneel down, tucking Maddy's hand below her cheek, giving her what little comfort I can as the magic takes hold.

"Soon," I whisper my promise.

It will all be over soon.

Twenty-Two

Commander Alburn isn't even home while I pack my things, not that I expected him to be. I've only lived under his roof for more than ten years, grew up there. He taught me to fight in the grassy backyard, hours upon hours of swordplay, archery, until my face was bright red and my body covered in bruises. Never guns though. Those were reserved for the barracks. He never cared much for them. I wonder if that's why they quickly became my favorite weapon.

I sigh, looking at the empty walls of my childhood room. My paintings are the only things coming with me to the palace, my new home. I could not bear to let them go, couldn't imagine them growing dusty in the commander's attic. The very idea was wrong, made me squirm. The colors are too vibrant, the scenes too beautiful for such a fate. So I removed them from their frames, slightly guilty as I cut the canvases apart, and rolled them into a loose circle. The floppy cylinder now rests awkwardly in my arms.

I wonder what the queen will think when she sees me. Will she believe it an act of defiance? I'll make something up, an explanation. I've given too much up already.

My mother.

Asher.

Maddy

The rebels.

Even the other objects in my room feel like a loss. The wooden mirror with paint chips flaking off. The colorful glass vases along my window. I was even instructed to leave all of my clothes behind, that a brand new wardrobe awaits—full of bulky skirts and unruly dresses I'm sure. I already miss my pants, the jeans I spent hours scouring the old city for, finding a few pairs that fit just right. Patches line the seams, but the wear only makes them more comfortable.

No. I've given enough up. The paintings come with me. I will need something to dream of while I wait for the warm embrace of death.

With a final glance, I close the door and make my way to the carriage down below. If the driver thinks me strange, he does not react to the sight of my bulky cargo. He just opens the door and silently closes it behind me.

The journey ends too quickly and I arrive at the castle, greeted by another silent valet who leads me wordlessly through the dark maze of the palace, from halo to halo of candlelight, our steps echoing in the empty space.

We stop beside an ornate wooden door, already open, the first welcoming thing I've seen today. I wait in the entrance as he lights candles all around the room, bringing the space back to life. Large red curtains hang from ceiling to floor, completely opaque, blocking out the sun. The wooden bed frame is beautifully carved with flowers, culminating in an ornate canopy draped with silks. There are no books. The shelves rest empty, barren. A small vanity sits in the corner, pristine with a gold leaf mirror that looks hardly used. Has anyone even lived in this room before? Something about it feels lonely, deserted.

"Do you need anything else, my lady?"

It takes a second to realize he is speaking to me, though there is no one else around. I'm no lady.

"No." I shake my head and he leaves, closing the door behind him. When I am finally alone, a breath escapes my body, deep and tired. Alone once more, my shoulders droop, weary. The past few days have drained me. Gently, I place the paintings on my bed, leaving them for later, and tug open a curtain.

The effect is immediate. Light floods my dark room. The sun hits my skin, warming it, reenergizing me. Breathing easier, I pull the other half aside. As my eyes adjust to the brightness, I take in the view, disappointed. Fields and fields of green fill my vision. Beautiful. Wondrous. But not the old city, not the view I have stared at for most of my life, the one embedded in my soul.

I turn away, retreating into the scarlet box that surrounds me. The closet is full of silky dresses, jeweled and sparkly. The vanity has makeup I've never used and brushes that are encased in pearly opal. The shelves are indeed empty. But my paintings will hopefully make this room more familiar, more like home.

A knock sounds, distracting me. A moment later, the door opens.

"Jade, welcome home."

It's the queen. I'm unused to the cheer in her voice. I've never imagined it as anything but cold.

"Thank you," I murmur, trying to lace some excitement into the sound. "Everything is beautiful, Your Majesty."

She smiles warmly, stepping farther into my room. "There's no need for such formality, not anymore."

But I'm not sure how to respond, so I remain silent, watching her circle the small space, searching every nook. When her eyes land on the paintings covering my bed, she pauses, wrinkling her nose in distaste, but the expression passes quickly. I breathe a small sigh of relief.

My paintings have passed inspection.

"Come," she orders, taking my elbow in her hand and leading me to the vanity. Her touch brings bile to my throat, spins my stomach with nausea, as though my hatred is a physical disease. I force it down. I must act calm, detached, like the Jade she believes me to be.

With a little push, I sit in the chair, facing the mirror while the queen stands above me. The two of us could not look more different. I am dark where she is light. Brown hair. Tanned skin. Eyes blazing green and not blue. Still, there is something in the way our faces perch at the very top of our necks, strong and proud, that makes me feel we are not so different after all. The thought sends a fierce shiver down my spine, a fire scorching my skin, and I try my best not to squirm.

"I've always wanted a daughter," she murmurs as she pulls my hair back over my shoulders. Chilly fingers bring goose bumps to my neck before releasing my skin and reaching for the brush. "My mother and I used to sit like this every night preparing for dinner. She would brush my hair until it shined just like a candle flame. I was always amazed by her nimble touch, how she twisted and braided my hair into the most wonderful creations."

The brush slides through my waves, catching knots, but I keep my face still, free of pain. Did my mother brush my hair? I don't remember. It's hard to recall even what she looked like, the sound of her voice, the touch of her hands. All I recollect is the soft cocoon of safety that always sheltered me, kept me warm. I knew when she was there that I had nothing to fear.

Completely different from my life now.

Each new day brings a new terror. All because of the woman standing over me, touching me as though we are close, as though she has earned some privilege. And I must let her.

"As I got older, I would sit where you are, imagining that one day I would have a daughter who sat like a perfect princess while I twirled her hair."

I watch the queen in the mirror. Her eyes have grown softer, darker, filled with concentration as her fingers move in rhythm, up and down, up and down. The angles on her face don't seem quite as harsh. Is this the woman Asher would have known had he been born a girl? Could so small a detail really have made so large an impact?

"In a few days' time, we will be like family. The ceremony will connect us through magic you can't even begin to understand, but I will teach you how to wield it."

I bite my cheeks to keep from grinning. I have a timeline. In a few days' time, I will kill the queen. But I don't say that. Head downcast, I murmur, "I am excited to learn, Your Majesty."

Queen Deirdre pulls on my hair, braiding it, forcing my head back up. Our eyes meet in the reflection.

I pause, worried that she has read my thoughts, that she can sense the revulsion coursing through my veins, the pit of anger boiling in my chest.

But a wide smile spreads across her lips, maybe the first real one I've ever seen lighten her frosty features. "I would like you to call me Mother, Jade," she says, voice fragile. Do I dare say vulnerable?

In that moment, I understand two things very clearly.

First, that I truly am immune to the queen. Even her magic cannot crack the shell around my heart if she cannot sense that Mother is the last thing I would ever truly call her.

Second, that hope is a weapon even evil things cannot defeat. The gleam in her eye is unmistakable. She wants to believe that she is on the brink of making all of her dreams come true.

So I open my mouth. I say a word I never thought I would gift to her. But in it, I have sealed her fate. "Mother," I whisper, a small nervous smile on my lips, eyes shining bright—not out of joy, but out of victory.

Without her powers, the queen does not know the difference. She looks away, swallowing, but the grin comes back to her lips, giddy, almost girlish. "Good," she says, pinning my hair in a perfect knot atop my head and then stepping away. "I will see you later tonight for dinner. Wear one of your new dresses."

"I will," I say, and then I force one more word out just to drive the point home, "Mother."

After the queen is gone, it takes all of my willpower not to scream. Instead, I rip the pins from my hair, breathing heavily, shaking violently until my curls fall naturally once more.

I want nothing to do with her. I don't want her castle. I don't want her magic. I definitely don't want her affection. I ache to toss it all away. But I can't.

So instead, I stomp to the bed to retrieve my paintings. They will calm me. They will let me escape into daydreams just as they always have. But the canvases have rolled off my bed while the queen was here, as though afraid of her, so I bend, searching the floor until I spot them under the mattress. Reaching, I pull. But just beyond the bundle rests a little box tucked in the corner, almost hidden in the folds of the curtains. I grab it, intrigued.

This is just the distraction I needed.

A mystery.

I lift the wood onto my lap, running my fingers over the smooth edges. The dark stain is broken by a few hints of the natural grain hidden below. The carving is simple, just a rectangle with no extra grooves, no miniature sculptures or words. The only adornment is a little metal plate etched with the words, "For my son. To keep your dreams safe."

I ease open the lid, intrusive, wondering what secrets are stored inside, but all that waits are papers. Scrawls and crude pictures cover the pages. I reach in, lifting a small bundle loosely bound with string. The front cover reads, *The Lonely Prince and the Fearsome Dragon.*

I open the fragile page, trying not to bend the paper as I read the first few lines of the story. *Once there was a lonely prince who lived in a lonely palace all by himself.* The prince is drawn below, a big circle of a face, yellow squiggles for hair, eyes a bright purple. Suddenly I know who this is, even with the most childish of drawings, I understand.

Asher.

The box was his. The stories are his. What else was a boy to do, all alone in a castle with no friends, no mother who bothered to pay attention to him? The lonely prince…

My heart grows heavy. A tickle burns the back of my throat.

I should not be looking at these. They are too private. Too personal. Still, I cannot stop my fingers from turning the small page, reading what comes next.

His kingdom was under the spell of a fearsome dragon. No one remembered who they were. This page contains the image of a yellow dragon with bright blue eyes standing over the houses below. The identity of this character is all too obvious, even without the crown balanced on its forehead.

The queen.

I keep reading, ignoring the pictures, focusing on the story.

The lonely prince knew what he needed to do. He needed to slay the dragon and free his friends so no one was lonely anymore. So he found the dragon's lair and faced the fearsome dragon.

When the lonely prince began to charge, the dragon sat down. "I don't want to fight," she said. The dragon did not look so fearsome anymore. She looked lonely, like the prince.

The prince put down his sword. "Release my people," he said. But the dragon shook her head. "Then I'll be alone." The prince touched her long snout. "We can be alone together."

The prince and the dragon were never lonely again.

I close my eyes tight. My chest constricts painfully.

Oh Asher, what a beautiful dream.

I understand now why he hesitated, why he could not shoot. He never thought he would have to. Somehow, he always believed deep down in his soul that his mother was a good person, was as sad as he was, just needed a friend. He truly thought that given the chance she would do the right thing.

I want to cry for him. I wonder if he understands how close his dreams were, how different his life would have been had he been born a girl, that the only reason for his mother's hatred was something completely out of his control.

I dig through the papers, reading more titles. *The Lonely Prince and the Beautiful Princess. The Lonely Prince and the Long Lost King. The Lonely Prince and the Peasant Boy.* On and on they go, little bundles filled with the stories that Asher created, dreams a sad little boy was too afraid to speak out loud, confessions only paper could hold. Stories of redemption, of hope, of faith.

Stories of love.

I close the lid and push the box back under the bed, deep out of sight where it belongs. Where Asher wanted it. Safe from the eyes of his mother. But even as I stand, unroll my paintings, I can't remove the stories from my mind. They dig in, fight while I try to jostle them free, try not to think about Asher.

But it's no use.

A memory floods my vision. Asher holding my hand as the sinkhole opened below me, saving me, saving someone who did not deserve to be redeemed. A galaxy shimmered in his eyes, as they seemed to whisper that everything would be fine, that he would never let me go. And in the split second where the ground gave way, I believed him. My hand tightened on his, letting the warmth of his body embrace me. I trusted that he would keep his promise. And he trusted that I would become worthy of it.

Just like he trusted the queen.

As quickly as the image comes, it fades.

I stumble as though I've just been slapped, unsteady, breath coming heavy. My fingers tremble, my heart pounds. For the first time, I realize how deep my betrayal really was. Everything he ever believed was shattered, by me, by the queen. What if the boy I love is truly gone? What if together Queen Deirdre and I broke his faith?

I need to see Asher.

Now that I know the queen can no longer read my thoughts, can no longer touch my emotions, I need to explain. To apologize. He needs to understand.

I run from my room, urgency flooding my veins, tunneling my vision so I can hardly see. I don't even know where to go.

It doesn't matter.

I'll find him. I always do.

Twenty-Three

Asher is in the dungeon.

I searched the halls for almost an hour before I found myself stepping down, deeper into the mountain below the castle, circling round and round while the sunlight disappeared overhead. My eyes adjusted to the dark as my legs continued to descend, pulled by an invisible force. Now I watch him from the shadows, body curled behind an archway, stopped by fear.

What can I say to fix things?

Are there any words that might make it right?

Will he ever forgive me?

These are the thoughts that freeze my body, questions I am not sure I am prepared to answer, answers I am not sure my heart can bear to hear.

He looks the image of defeat, surrounded by a halo of candlelight. Shadows stripe his body, only enhancing the fact that he is behind bars. With knees bent, his torso curls into his legs while his head hangs limp in between, staring at the floor. The subtle rise and fall of his back is the only indicator that he is alive. Everything else seems numb.

"Asher?" I call, voice carrying loudly through the silence.

He does not stir.

I close the space between us, hands grasping cold iron rods, wishing I could break in and touch his warm skin, kiss it back to life.

"Why?" he whispers, harsh.

I know what he's asking, and I won't play games with his emotions, not anymore. "I refused to let you die."

His hand slams against the floor, a slap that echoes off the walls.

I flinch.

"That was never your choice to make," Asher growls, head whipping up, fury evident in his bloodshot eyes laced with bright red veins. Dirt covers his face, caked by sweat. His luminescent blond hair is flat, pressed down so I can almost see the grooves where his fingers have rested day after day, holding his heavy head.

He still looks beautiful to me. And I ache to wrap my arms around him.

"Asher," I murmur, pleading.

"No, Jade, it was my choice. My destiny. And now, everything I've spent my entire life preparing for is gone." His tone grows quieter, hushed. A subtle change spreads over his face. His jaw loosens, unclenching, bringing his cheeks down, unflaring his nostrils. The angular squint around his eyes disappears, smoothes over, and then reappears, softer, downcast. Asher's head falls back, knocking against the wall as his gaze travels to the ceiling.

"I failed," he whispers, as though he's forgotten I'm even here. "I couldn't do it."

I reach a hand through the bars, as though to touch him, to comfort him. "It'll be okay—"

"How?" He interrupts, voice dark. "The rebel army marches on a queen who is very much alive, who will capture them, who will destroy them all because of me."

I hesitate, but then push through. I need to be honest, for once in my life. "Actually, they're already here. The queen already has them under her thrall."

He sniggers, an exhale drenched in sarcasm. "Great, just great. Everyone is trapped, and the only person who can free them is stuck down here behind bars." He shrugs, looking around the small space, shaking his head. "What a hero I turned out to be."

"You're wrong, Asher," I urge. "You are the hero, and that's why you couldn't shoot. You're too good a person. These people don't need a hero."

He meets my gaze. "Then what do they need?"

"They need a killer." I take a deep breath. "They need me."

The air between us suddenly evaporates, sharpens,

and the distance disappears. His eyes seem no more than an inch away, expanding, taking over my vision as they entrap me, hold me captive. I can't breathe. I'm growing lightheaded under his scrutiny, under the intensity of his stare.

"What do you mean?" He says each word slowly, separately, emphasizing each syllable.

"I'm going to kill the queen," I whisper, worried that somehow, somewhere, she can hear me.

Asher's brows pull together tightly as his head cocks slightly to the side. "Why? What will that get you? I'll just…" His eyes begin to widen as his voice trails off. "What did you do?"

My mouth goes dry.

Asher stands, slowly, stretching like a panther hunting his prey. Each step he takes causes my heart to pound, to jump so that it might burst from my chest.

"Jade," he presses, movements still calm, purposeful. I release the bars, stepping backward, out of reach until my shoulders hit the damp wall behind me and I am stuck, pinned down by the daggers shooting from his eyes.

"I'm sorry, Asher," I whisper. Perhaps this is my real betrayal. The thing that will hurt him most. But I need to tell him. I need him to understand.

He grips the cell, shaking. "What did you do?"

"I never wanted to hurt you," I say. Now that I've started, the words bubble up like a great storm, spilling from my lips. "I just wanted to save your life, and I knew, I knew there was something we were missing. Some route we were too ignorant to see. And I was right. You don't have to die, Asher."

I pause, unsure if I can continue, what will happen if I do, if I finally tell him the complete truth.

"Say it," he whispers, desperation straining his voice, roughing up his words. Pain pulls at his cheeks.

I give in.

"Queen Deirdre is going to make me her heir. I'm going to take your place."

I thought he might yell.

Might scream.

Might fight.

But this is worse. This pervasive silence. Asher stops, mouth dropping open in disbelief. The color drains from his face. Fingers that were holding tight to his cage release, drop slowly to his side. Then he dips, bending at the knees until they land hard against the stone floor. All his will has been stripped free from his muscles.

"She knows a spell that will transfer the magic to me," I continue, needing to fill the void opening wide between us. "I'm not sure what it entails, but in a few days' time, it will be done. I'll kill the queen. I'll kill myself. And then you and everyone else will be free."

"No." He looks up, standing, pacing. "I won't let you."

"You can't stop me." I shake my head, apologetic.

"I will. I'll…" Asher's eyes roam the walls as though searching for the answer, flicking up and down, side to side, landing back on me. "I'll tell her your plan. I'll tell her what you're going to do."

"And what would that accomplish?" I ask, even toned. "The queen will kill me for betraying her, and you'll still be stuck down here."

"Then I'll kill her before she can complete the spell," he urges.

"How? From your cell?"

He opens his mouth, closes it, runs a hand through his hair. "I'll free myself. I'll rip the door off its hinges. I don't know, but I'll find a way."

"Asher." I sigh, closing the gap between us. Gently, I grab his hands, breathing in the heat from his fingers. Electricity flares below our skin, sparks the air around us, as though at any moment we might catch fire. I wish that I could erase the bars between us, that I could curl into his chest. I crave the feel of his arms circling my waist, holding me close, making me forget everything except us.

A smile spreads my lips, crinkles the corners of my eyes. I wasn't sure if I would ever touch him again. But now, as passion burns through our palms, I wonder how I ever thought a flame this strong could fade out.

Our lips wait torturously close.

"I never should have brought you to the rebel camp," he confesses. Anguish softens the words until they feel fragile, about to break. "It's all my fault. If we never met—"

"Don't." I squeeze.

He ignores the plea, finishing his thought. "If we never met, you never would have put yourself in this position."

I dip my head, search for the eyes he has pointed at the ground. I find them. I see the stars again, glittering from the candlelight, dancing just for me.

"I would have." And I sense the truth in the words as I say them. "Somehow, someway, I would have ended up here. This is what I was born to do, Asher, I can feel it. But because I met you, I can say that I lived before I died. For a brief few weeks of my life, I felt. I grieved. I yearned. I—"

Loved.

But Asher's lips have stolen the word, snatched it from the air, buried it deep within his heart.

I don't mind.

It belonged to him anyway.

It lives in this kiss. Tangible in the caress of his fingers as they travel up my spine, grip the back of my neck and pull me closer. Alive in the velvet brush of his lips as they tease, drift away, smash closer, a tantalizing tide. Palpable in the bliss of our sighs as they rise, sheltering us the from the real world waiting just a few stories above.

Cool metal presses into my cheekbones as I strain to

be closer, to feel my body touch every piece of his. The firm muscles in his biceps, the soft hairs tickling the silky skin of his neck. I use my hands to explore because I know in my heart that this is goodbye, that this is the last time the heat from his lips will fill my veins, surging through me like an immense wave, removing all thought, all control.

Asher knows it too.

His kiss becomes frantic, pecking my chin, my cheeks, my nose. Every inch of my face that he can touch becomes wrapped in those lips that I do not want to leave behind. I don't even realize I'm crying until the taste of his mouth grows salty. My body starts to tremble, my breath to shake. I wobble, unsteady on my feet.

Asher stops, leans back, face wet with my tears.

"We'll find a way, Jade," he whispers.

I lick my lips, trying to regain control over my wayward senses. "There is no other way, Asher. You know, you were prepared to do it yourself."

"Well," he says, breathing deep, eyes growing dark, "I was an idiot."

The tension breaks. We both release sad laughter, weak, lined with bitter joy. I sniffle, swallowing the grief back down to fester unseen until I cannot ignore it anymore.

"Yes, you were." I grin, blinking the water from my eyes. "But not about this."

"There was a gaping flaw in my plan, something I didn't realize until you flipped it around on me." He brings his palm to my cheek, holding it, wiping the water away. "I don't want to live without you. So you see, there has to be another way."

"Not so easy to be the one left behind, is it?" I tease. Joking makes everything seem easier. Less real. Less permanent.

Asher shrugs, putting his brave face on for my benefit. "What do I know? I didn't even realize that a new heir could be chosen, could be spelled into the role. Who says there's no other way to release the magic back into the world?"

"Asher," I say, more serious. I won't let him sway me from what I must do. I don't want him to believe in a false hope. I of all people understand how dangerous that can be. Wishing for freedom, my unattainable dream, is what brought me into this whole mess in the first place.

"All I'm saying is don't do anything stupid. We'll figure it out together."

I could fight him. Force him to understand. But I don't want to.

In my soul, I know that these are the last few precious moments of alone time Asher and I will ever share. The only ones we'll ever have that are not tied up with hidden truths, shaded by lies. Our hearts are open, honest. No darkness lurks in the corners of our minds.

For the first time, all our secrets have been bared.

And Asher loves me regardless.

I loop my fingers between the buttons of his shirt, tugging him gently closer. He understands. The humor in his gaze fades, turns to a smolder. Lavender fire blazes to life in his eyes.

I melt, putty in his hands.

Twenty-Four

I hardly recognize myself as I look in the mirror. The queen has pinned my hair elegantly away from my face, folding and sculpting it into a waterfall cascading down my back. The makeup I have ignored for the better part of a week glistens in the candlelight. Black liquid lines my eyes, gold highlights glitter my lids, soft rouge sparkles along my cheekbones, and ruby red paints my lips. A maid has helped button the pearls stretching down my spine, cinching the red folds of my dress tightly around my waist.

I look like a princess.

I look like her.

There is one difference though. I smirk as my hand travels to my thigh, lightly patting the gun I've strapped across my muscle. The ceremony is tonight. Queen Deirdre still has not told me what it entails, what I must do. All I know is that I am to meet her in the west tower at sunset.

The servant has been gone for an hour, giving me time to steel my nerves, to contemplate every terrible thing the queen has done, to ready myself to take her life and then my own. My heart flutters painfully, fighting against my mind, telling me there might be another way. Hopeful.

I turn from the mirror, squashing that desire, ignoring it. Pink streaks have just appeared outside my window, stretching lightly across the sky, shadowing the blue, turning it darker. Under any other circumstances, the scene would be beautiful, a real life painting I might admire. But tonight, it is the last pieces of sand dropping through the hourglass, telling me that time has run out.

Just as the thought enters my mind, a knock sounds lightly on my door. With one deep breath, I expel my tension, bringing a warm excited smile to my lips.

"Good evening, my lady," the servant says, bowing deeply as I open the door.

"Good evening," I reply, voice light.

Without another word exchanged, he begins to walk down the halls and I follow. After a few nights in the castle, I am used to the routine. We do not speak—we're not supposed to. I tried at first, but quickly realized how uncomfortable the man became, face red, hands squirming, lips drawn thin.

Tonight, I enjoy the silence, letting my thoughts wander to Asher, to my mother, to the rebels. Everyone I will help with my sacrifice. The images form a warm bubble in my chest, fighting the fear knotting my stomach, helping control it.

The bubble bursts as shouts flicker down the staircase looming overhead. I begin to climb, step after step, circling up the steep tower. My feet wish to run, but I must stay calm, I must keep pace with the servant. The higher we climb, the clearer the voice becomes.

I close my eyes tight, biting my inner cheeks to keep from whimpering.

Asher.

"Mother!" His voice echoes in the space around me, bouncing off old stone. "Mother, what are you doing? Don't do this!"

I try to tune him out, to pretend that I don't care, to keep up my front. But with each new outburst, my hands tremble. For some reason, I didn't think he'd be here. I hoped we could do the spell without him. I thought maybe he wouldn't need to see me as a monster, as a killer.

I blink rapidly, clearing my eyes as we reach the landing and step into the small room. The walls are lined with books, the only ones I've seen in the castle. Curtains are draped all around, blocking out the walls, removing any windows except for the singular skylight overhead. Through the break in the stone, I see a deep purple sky and the barest outline of a luminescent moon. Full, completely round.

In the center of the room, Asher wrestles with the commander as he is strapped into a chair, chained there. He meets my stare. I try to look away, to remain unaffected by his presence, but I don't miss the hint of failure in his eyes. He really thought he could break free, that he might stop me from completing my plan.

I tear my eyes away.

"Jade, listen to me," Asher shouts, "there's another way. I found another way."

Pain pricks my heart but I refuse to give in, to listen. Asher would say anything to stop me, anything, but his protests will only make all of this harder. I tune him out as my gaze finds the woman standing a few feet behind him, dressed almost the same as me except for the metal crown resting on her head.

"Gag him," she orders and Asher's shouts muffle, drowning in his throat because they cannot penetrate the cloth shoved into his mouth. The queen pays no attention, walking gracefully around him, skirt sashaying toward me as she takes my hand.

"Jade," she says, voice warm, affectionate.

"Mother." I squeeze her fingers, relieved when my voice comes out completely smooth, almost natural. Asher's eyes go wide with shock. I fight not to meet his questioning glance. "I've been eagerly waiting for this day to come."

"And it's finally here, after what feels like a lifetime."

You have no idea, I want to say, to sneer. But my lips remain in a tight smile. I nod my head in Asher's direction, nose upturned. "Does he have to be here?"

The queen pats my hands, as though I am her pet. "I'm afraid yes, for the ceremony. But afterward I will be done with my son, and you may do with him what you may."

"Good," I say, infusing as much disdain as I can into my voice. But in reality, my chest feels light, and I breathe easily for the first time in hours. The ceremony will not kill him and that is all I needed to hear to carry on.

"Just sit down." The queen leads me to the empty chair resting opposite Asher. I carefully spread my dress, hoping to give an air of actually caring that it does not wrinkle as I ease down. Forced to look at him, I do not miss the pleading waves Asher sends my way. He is shaking his head, no longer at his mother, but at me. The tendons in his neck pull taught against his restraints, bulging as he tries to find the air to speak, to fill his voice. The words come out dull, muted, unclear.

For once, I'm glad he has been quieted.

I look over his shoulder at the commander as he tightens Asher's binds and steps away, back to his queen. We have not spoken since I left his house, and I doubt he will say anything now. What will he do when I kill the queen? When I become the one with the power? Will he be the one who kills me, or will the transfer be so quick that I will gain his instant loyalty?

I'm not sure I like either option, so I look away, at the floor in front of my toes, gold slippers barely visible under my skirt. Asher's eyes are like lasers on my skin, burning so that it almost feels as though he sees past the clothes to my skin below. I wonder if he thinks I look beautiful, or if I look like a clone of the woman he has hated and loved for his entire life.

"I have not told you very much about the ceremony," the queen says, walking to the shelves on the wall and pulling a small pouch free. "But I will explain a little bit now. Under the light of the full moon, I will mix your blood with my son's and through that bond, the magic will transfer, sinking under your skin until it bleeds free of his. There is nothing you need to do except sit and remain calm while I work."

My stomach flips, rocketing into my throat before tumbling back down. I nod, unable to find words.

Her cold fingers find my skin, brushing over my forehead, then my bare shoulder, trying to soothe. "It will all be over soon," she whispers.

Yes.

It will.

Resting the pouch on a small table, the queen removes a sharp needle and a vial of silvery powder. I swallow.

"Your hand," she asks, and I offer it willingly. I do not flinch as the metal pierces my skin, bringing a line of ruby red blood to the surface. As it continues to run, the queen sprinkles a small dusting of the powder overtop and the blood on my hand thickens, turning to a paste, no longer about to drip off of my palm.

"Asher," she says, looking at him as though he were vermin. But Asher shakes his head, mumbling through the gag, muscles clenching to disobey. The commander steps forward, grasping his forearm and flipping it over. With his biceps bound to the back of the chair, Asher has no chance to stop him, so he watches, protests growing louder as the needle punctures his skin and the powder solidifies his blood.

Knowing what I must do without being told, I instinctually reach forward, resting my palm over his, connecting the wounds. Our blood bonds so our fingers are glued together, stuck. There is no turning back now. I don't think there ever was.

Asher squeezes my hand tight, trying to get me to look at him, to listen, to stop. But my head is clear. I welcome the ending to my story. I'm ready.

The commander steps back and the queen circles us, dropping the powder in a ring around our chairs as she goes. In the moonlight, it glows, a faint luminescence that rises from the floor, sparkling.

The queen begins to murmur words I can't quite hear, too soft to understand, but the radiance around us grows, rising higher, pulsing brighter. The light blinds my eyes, encasing Asher and me, surrounding us and blocking out the room, the castle, the village below, as though the moon has fallen free of the sky and swallowed us inside of it.

I see nothing except him, eyes just like the sky we left behind. The corners are crinkled, furious and sad at the same time.

Asher.

The word haunts my lips, but I do not speak it just in case the queen can still hear. Just in case our solitude is an illusion, another magic spell meant to trick us. My thumb traces the curve of his palm, gently brushing his skin, doing what my lips cannot. His gaze softens.

The bond between our palms tightens, pulled by an invisible force that stretches up my arm, straining underneath my muscles, spreading ever further. The power tugs on my heart, yanking, using the beat to pulse through the rest of my body. Down to the tops of my toes, the magnet stretches, suctioning until my whole body is alert, on edge, taut. The veins in my limbs go empty as my blood is sucked away and I begin to grow cold.

I go blind.

My heart stops beating.

My fingers turn numb.

My breath dissolves in my lungs.

I can no longer feel Asher's warmth, his touch. I am floating in the emptiness.

Then all at once my eyes go wide, and I am thrown back against my chair as heat fills my skin, runs up my arm and into my heart, pumping, spreading, filling my empty corpse and bringing life back to my body. Blood surges up my arm, foreign and familiar, laced with a fire I have never felt before. I gulp in a breath, reborn.

The force of the transfer presses against my body, tugging Asher and me apart. The chair beneath me moves, an inch, and then two, then three. I am bent in half, hand still connected to Asher, but my waist is flying in the opposite direction so that I might split down the middle at any second.

I scream as pain rips my shoulder. My eyes go white. I'm worried my arm is gone, lost, but as I blink clear, I realize I am still intact. Barely. The tendons in my bicep start to tear. The nerves blaze. Tears spring to my eyes.

And then we snap.

My back slams into a bookcase as I am hurled across the room and then drop to the floor. Eyes snapping up, I find Asher. His chair is broken in bits around him, and the chains binding him have loosened. But he does not move, does not fight to free his limbs.

Asher is still.

Immobile.

Eyes closed. I am not even sure if he is breathing.

I yearn to slink across the room, to run to him, but a second awareness pulls at my mind, distracting me, blossoming and pushing all other thoughts aside. A tether springs to life in my chest, a little string growing stronger by the second. I follow the invisible line. My eyes do not need to see the connection to know where it leads. I sense it, hovering before me, stretching across the small room, ending not with Asher, but with the queen.

An aura surrounds her body, bright, like the glow that surrounded Asher and me.

The magic.

I can see it. Swirls of sparkles pulsing around her body, waves stretching from her skin and crashing against me, connecting us.

The ceremony worked.

I'm the heir.

I know it as well as I know my own name.

Jade.

Heir.

Two become one as the magic crawls inside of me, grounding itself, finally home. The cut on my hand has healed, sealed shut in the shape of a circle, a wheel spinning beneath my skin. Even that redness begins to fade as the magic swells, leaving no sign that nature has been altered.

"Jade."

I look up at the sound of my name.

The queen approaches, smiling wide, eyes warm as her hand stretches for mine. Half of my fingers itch to grasp her, to hold her, to call her Mother. But my right hand, not yet touched by the magic, dips below my skirts, following the line of my leg until it hits cool metal.

The gun.

I grip the handle, pulling it out of the strap as my pointer finger finds the trigger. Unsteady, I lift the weapon free of hiding. The safety is clicked off as I cock the gun, aiming, getting ready to fire.

"Don't come any closer," I growl, voice shaking just like my arm.

The queen stops.

The smile on her lips falters, twitches, sinking slowly into a frown. Her pale face drains of all color, becoming ghostly white as though a phantom stands before me. The hand she outstretched for an embrace recoils, fingers bending inward, cupped against her chest as her brow knots in confusion.

"Jade?"

In that question, I no longer hear the queen. I no longer see her. Instead, a little girl sprouts before my eyes, blond, sad—lonely just like the prince I have learned to love. Her mother held no love, just like her mother before her, and her mother before her, a long line of lonely royals all using magic to fill the void, not realizing that all it did was push people farther away.

The queen was human once, I know in that moment, in the shake of her voice, the vulnerability of confusion, the hurt of betrayal. And a small part of her still is. Behind the frozen façade rests a woman who wishes for a daughter, who thought perhaps she had finally found one in me. It's the woman Asher believed in, the one capable of hope, maybe even of love. The one he wanted beyond all things to redeem.

Shoot!

I scream, yelling at my finger to dip a little lower, to pull just a little tighter, to end the queen who stole so much from me. But her blue eyes no longer seem icy. The shade seems sad, isolated, completely alone. An empty sky without even a cloud to call a friend.

My muscles tense.

My entire body begins to shake.

I can do this.

I must do this.

But I hesitate. I wait just one second too long and a knife slashes my wrist, cutting deep, drawing blood. The gun clangs uselessly to the ground as I hiss in pain, turning to see the commander draw his sword back for another swing.

The world comes rushing back full force, color imploding in my eyes as my chest rips bare, exposed.

I failed.

The silver sword gleams as the commander raises it high overhead. I'm going to die.

No.

I step back as memories flood my mind. Every tactic I know, I learned from this man. The tower fades from my eyes. The queen and Asher are gone. The commander and I are alone, surrounded by soft grass, and he looms at least two feet overhead. I'm a girl once more, training in our backyard, learning the art of escape. Over and over, we would play. The commander always approached me the same way, blade high overhead, waiting to snap down, letting gravity add to his strength.

Back then, the weapon was made from wood, but right now, his blade shines with a deadly metal edge. He stops before me. My back has hit the wall, so I have nowhere else to run.

Steady, I hold my breath. Each move must be perfectly timed if I'm to beat him at his own game. So I wait for the secret I discovered as a girl, the little signal the commander never realized he sent out.

There. His arms hitch, inching back just a little farther, bringing the sword as far back as it will go, and he holds his breath.

I lunge to the side in the same second the commander brings his sword down, wincing as the metal slashes through the air right beside my ear, hissing with anger.

Stumbling in my skirts, I fall, yearning for the freedom of pants as I land hard against the ground. My torso twists as my hands search desperately for the gun.

My fingers clutch the handle and I snap up, meeting the commander's eyes. His face is as recognizable as my own, clearer in my mind than even my mother's. I've looked upon it for ten years and have never seen it so furious, so determined. He creeps forward, raising the sword once more, and two thoughts filter through my brain.

This man raised me. He trained me.

I don't hesitate as I put a bullet in his kneecap.

The commander falls to the ground with a howl. Perhaps in his old world swords were enough, but not in this world. Watching him hold a bloody hand to his wound, I cringe. I always told him to carry a gun, but he never believed he would need one. I'm not sure he really understood how deadly they could be.

I hold my finger over the trigger, unsure, and then drop the weapon.

I came here to kill, but not to kill him.

I can't.

Instead, I kick his sword away and slam the butt of the gun into his head, knocking him out. The commander will live. He'll hate me, but that is a consequence I will happily endure.

Five bullets left.

I stand, turning to the queen, determined to follow through on my fate.

The lonely little girl is gone.

In her place, the haughty queen I promised myself I would kill. Her lips are upturned, her hands clap in the silence, but anger seethes to life, ice blue flames in her eyes.

I raise the gun.

"Well done, Jade," the queen drawls, voice bitter, sharp. "I am not so easily fooled, but it seems you found my weakness."

I remain silent.

I know I should shoot, but I have the irrational desire to hear her out, to see if maybe, just maybe she will say the words I desperately want to hear, the one I promised myself I would forget as soon as Asher whispered them.

But a flame sparks to life in my chest, whispering that maybe somehow, someway, the two of us might be together. That maybe there is another way.

Hope.

That cruel fire.

That weapon no one can fight.

I pause.

"I'm impressed. You are more ruthless than I even guessed—a perfect trait for a queen."

"You would know," I spit. My finger inches tighter on the metal, trigger straining to be set free.

"Yet you can't shoot." The queen shrugs. No fear tightens her face. She is perfectly calm, collected. "I know why."

I swallow, throat dry, as her eyes shift to the side, to her sleeping son. He has not awoken from the spell, has not moved. But his cheeks are alive with color, peach, not the ashen gray of death.

My hope billows, swells wider.

"There is only one reason you would do what you've done, the same silly emotion I wanted to free you from, the most dangerous of them all." The queen sneers, unable to say it, as though the very thought creates a blockage in her throat. "Love."

I release a bullet.

It ricochets off the stone, falling uselessly to the ground.

The queen does not even flinch.

"Love is what freed me from you," I whisper, pulling the trigger tight again. This time I won't miss.

"But it won't be enough to free him," she says softly, eyes still on Asher.

My head explodes with shock. I drop the gun a hint. "What do you mean?"

"Magic has sent my son into a deep sleep, and only magic can wake him."

"How?"

The queen just laughs, looking at me with pity. "My dear Jade, do you really think I would tell you?"

I wave the gun, threatening, but her expression does not change. Mine morphs, falls, tightens.

"Put that gun down before you do something you might regret," she urges, voice silky as it sinks under my skin, forcing my hand to sink further, to let go of the trigger, to give in.

There is no magic in her words. I am immune. Good old fashion coercion moves me, it is the same method I've been using, the sort that takes a person's hope and twists it into steel.

I glance at Asher.

"I'm sorry," I whisper. And I am. Sorry that though I tried, I could not save him. That despite my efforts, Asher will die. But at least now, he will not do it alone.

The queen misunderstands me, grinning wide, clasping her hands in triumph. Her expression freezes that way as the bullet strikes her temple, sinking in, clearing the life from her eyes. The force throws her backward, into a curtain that crumples, exposing a hidden window.

Queen Deirdre's lifeless body tumbles through, disappearing into the night sky that looks so much like the eyes I will never see again, eyes that I will recognize for the rest of my short life.

I raise the gun to my head.

But before I can shoot, a different bullet strikes, plunging from the inside out. A bomb explodes in my chest, seizing my body, freezing it solid.

The magic.

And I am helpless against it.

Twenty-Five

An avalanche pulls me under until I am drowning in snow. So cold. I fall knees first to the ground, utterly silent, unable to release the scream trapped in my chest.

Pain explodes down my arms and legs. My ribs snap apart, as though opening wide, welcoming, and lightning strikes my heart, zapping my veins. I shake, seizing as pinpricks spread through my body, numbing it, disconnecting my brain.

Electric fire grows underneath my skin, funneling in from the sky, spreading wide. The ice begins to thaw, to melt away, replaced with lava that turns my insides to molten rock. I harden, turn to stone. My chest seals closed, the fire stops, and I hang in a void, not quite in the world but not quite out of it.

All I see are flashes of brilliant light in the dark, bursting overhead, bursting internally. Little explosions tear my organs apart and then replace them with something new, something not wholly human, something that yearns to be set free.

A force is alive inside of me.

The magic, I realize, but it has a will, like a spirit who wishes to escape. My veins are chains, holding it down, holding it captive. Power seeps through my skin, released into the world where it wishes to be, but the essence remains locked in my heart, pounding with each beat, hoping someone besides me might hear it.

But no one can.

My eyes ease open, greeted by the stones in the ceiling above. I sit up, muscles aching.

How much time has passed?

I have no idea. But it could not have been long.

I look around the room. The commander rests immobile in the corner, still unconscious from the blow to his head. Blood pours from the hole in his knee. But it is not the wound that grips my attention, it is the subtle neon glow around his body, putrid yellow mixed with hot lime green, raw pain, raw distress. Inside his chest, a white star gleams, pulsing with a slow beat. His soul or his heart? Or are those one and the same? I'm not sure.

I stand, pulled over by curiosity, by a new instinct blossoming to life. Placing my hand to his cheek, I kneel and suck in a breath. The magic flares to life in my veins, urging me to use it, to let go. The energy under my fingers grows until it stings. I give in.

Emotions flood my system. Pain. Fear. Hurt. Longing. Love. I coerce them into my bloodstream, feeling everything, stealing the sensations from his body. I am warmed by them, made more human by them. The aura surrounding the commander fades away. His eyes lose their crinkle, easing open, calmed despite the wound. He is empty, but his breath comes easier. The star in his chest brightens to a pure white, no longer damped by the colorful array of emotions surrounding his figure.

Easing back onto my heels, I rip his shirt, shredding the cloth to tie a tourniquet around the wound. The commander will be fine, especially now that his panic has been stripped away. But I look away, unable to look at him knowing what I've just done, how similar to the queen I have become.

The spirit inside of me subdues, no longer pulling against me for freedom, but rather content to ride the humanity I have fed it. With the magic under control, reality sinks back in. Memories flood my system.

"Asher!"

I bolt up, revolving until I find his still body on the floor, and then I run to him. A star beams from his heart, strong, almost blinding. But a subtle black shadow surrounds his limbs, seeps into his skin. Death. Decay. Yet his chest rises and falls.

Trapped within the gloom, he is alive.

I put a hand to his cheek, but the magic recoils,

shrugs back in fear—it will not accept this gift. The power only wants promises of life, and all Asher exudes is mortality. I pull anyway. The darkness does not move except to cling to Asher tighter.

"Come on," I beg, yanking, trying to force the magic into submission. The queen said it would heal him. That magic was the only thing that could cure him.

Did I really think it could be so easy?

I take a different method, shaking his shoulders. "Asher!" I shout, as though I can pull him from this sleep through determination alone. "Wake up!"

No movement crosses his eyes or his lips. His hands fall lifeless to the floor, limp, and his head rolls to the side. I follow the ghostly gaze, eyes slipping across the floor to the gun resting a few feet away, pointed at me, speaking for the prince.

I know what Asher would want me to do. Though he said we would find another way, we both knew the truth. Asher wants the magic released back to the wilds where it belongs. There is only one way to do it. Still, my fingers caress his soft cheek, unprepared to say goodbye, to leave him like this.

I stand, eyes shifting to the window where the queen drew her last breath, mind sinking to the sleepy town below. Self-loathing spews from my gut with each step closer, but I do not stop moving until my palms grip the stones. I lean out, wind billowing against my cheeks, and gasp.

Sky and land mirror each other, each an ebony blanket dusted with stars. Above, the stars are a million miles away. Below, they are all too close, prickling my heart with awareness.

The queen described this to me once, tried to show me. Back then, I didn't fully understand why, but I do now. An entire universe is splayed out before me, sparkling dots connecting into a million constellations, each one centered around me. Their hearts are beacons calling out. The magic inside my limbs answers, pulsing down below to take their troublesome emotions away, leaving them pure, untainted with humanity.

I can live a thousand different lives in the span of one. Everything they experience, I do too. Everything they feel floods my veins. But right now, I only want to find one life, one person who I promised I would not use, but who I must. The only person I trust to do right by Asher's body, to not give up on him after I am gone, to try to nurse him back to health.

Maddy.

As soon as her name enters my thoughts, one star brightens, overtaking the others, and in my head a new awareness springs. I sense her emotions, the confusion bubbling beneath her skin, a sadness. I close my eyes and behind those lids, I see what she sees. Wooden walls, bales of hay, soft black hairs beneath her fingers. She is in a stable, petting a horse slowly, softly.

I tug on the magic.

She stops moving.

I yank again.

Maddy's head lifts.

I steal her thoughts, her emotions, emptying her mind, and bring a new idea to fruition. The castle. Hurry.

When my eyes open, her star is moving swiftly through the streets. Horse hooves echo in my ears, carrying her quickly to me. The magic fizzes, excited to be used, but I form my hands into fists, hating how natural this feels, and release Maddy from my head.

I have a few minutes, fifteen or twenty at the most.

I must be gone by the time she gets here.

The commander still has not woken, leaving Asher and me, for the most part, alone. I sit beside him, lifting his head gently onto my lap, brushing stray hairs off his forehead.

The magic will not disappear from my sight, so I must look beyond it to see the boy I love. Underneath the black shadow that encases him, I find my prince. The soft curves of his face. The straight nose barely dusted with freckles. The light brown lashes that perfectly frame his closed eyes. I yank the gag from his lips and Asher breathes easier, mouth open just slightly, almost inviting.

Leaning down, I brush my lips softly against his. They are warm, but motionless, and I pull away, searching his face once more. For a moment, I allow myself to think he might wake, just like in the stories. But Asher does not move. Does not blink.

My kiss is not enough to save him.

I dip closer to his ear. Though I know the words will not penetrate his slumber, I must say them. We waited too long. I always thought they would be too painful to hear, too painful to say, especially when I knew they would only be temporary. But I whisper them anyway.

"I love you."

My heart feels lighter as soon as I speak. The magic in my chest buzzes, waiting, listening as though it is just as invested in the response as I am.

Silence is all that greets us.

I press on, throat stinging, eyes wet. "I know you didn't want to say goodbye, so maybe this is for the best. When you wake up, everything will be like you always dreamed it would be. Everyone will be free. You'll be their hero, and they'll love you."

A tear drops from my eye, staining his cheek. I wipe it away with my thumb, sniffling the rest back in.

"I don't want you to blame yourself. There was no way you could have stopped me, could have stopped this. I just want you to live, to be happy, to find love. I want to give you everything that you gave me. In the old world, people used to think the dead watched over us. My mother used to tell me that my father was looking down on me, proud of me, keeping me safe. I'm not sure if I believe that, but I do know that if I can, I'll keep my eyes locked on you. I'll protect you."

I lay Asher down, removing the chains from his body, brushing all of the broken bits of chair away from him. I tear the bottom foot of my skirt off, bunching the silk into a pillow, and set his head gently down.

The shadow over his body looks a little grayer, a little less opaque. I pray its because he's getting better. That the magic is somehow doing its job.

I'll never know for sure.

Easing back onto my feet, I grab the gun on my way up. I want to tell him I love him one more time. I want to whisper goodbye. But I can't. A plug blocks my throat, making it difficult to even breathe. My eyes have blurred.

I turn away, facing the window, unable to look at him while I do this. I met Asher at the dangerous end of gun, and as I press the barrel against the side of my head, I realize I will say goodbye the same way.

I don't want to die. Not really. Not if I had a choice. All I've ever wanted is to live, to be free. But I think of all the stars twinkling on the ground below me, souls trapped in the magic coursing through my veins, and I understand what I must do.

I don't fear death.

I fear life, this life I have found myself in. I fear being queen. I fear what will happen to me if I do not let them go, if I put myself first. I fear the way Asher will look at me if he wakes to find me alive, turned into the mother he could not kill. I fear the hatred that would burn in his eyes.

Taking a deep breath, I begin my countdown.

One.

My heart sinks just a little.

Two.

I tighten my fingers on the gun.

Three.

I pull the trigger.

Twenty-Six

"Jade!"

Is death so quick? Has Asher come to welcome me at the gates of heaven? Or have I been banished to hell, cursed to hear his voice in my head for all eternity, knowing I will never touch him again?

A warm hand lands on my cheek. Darkness surrounds me. But it gradually fades as fingers dig into my shoulders, shaking me. Asher continues to call my name.

"Jade!"

"Can you hear me?"

"Jade!"

Pain explodes in my forehead, a sharp point just above my ear. But despite it, I begin to laugh, to cry, to weep. All at the same time. I am alive.

What a bitter realization that is as Asher's face becomes clearer, looking down into my eyes, worry evident on his features. I blink. He lifts me into his arms, hugging me into his chest, crying, laughing too. But I know his sighs are ones of relief. Mine are of dread. I'm not sure if I can pull that trigger again, not now, not when Asher is looking at me with love in his eyes.

"What happened?" I murmur, awed, confused.

"The gun misfired," he tells me, ripping it from my hands and tossing it to the far side of the room. "But the barrel still slammed into your skull from the kickback and knocked you down. I was so scared, Jade, I thought you were dead."

Asher pulls back, flattening my hair to my head, looking at me as though I might crumble at any moment, as though part of him believes I'm a ghost. But through the magic, I watch as his aura begins to change, from the deep purple of relief to a maroon filled with love to a brilliant red ripe with anger.

I wince.

"You said you wouldn't do anything stupid, you promised," Asher scolds, face harsh in the candlelight. "You almost shot yourself. If not for a mechanical malfunction, you'd be dead. What do you call that?"

"Honorable," I murmur. The red-hot blaze around him only ignites brighter. Before he can open his mouth to yell, I ask, "How are you awake? The queen said only magic could revive you."

Asher rolls his eyes. "As usual, the queen lied. I got knocked out when I hit the wall. I think I have a concussion or something, the room is spinning quite a bit actually. I thought I was just reeling in anger, but now I'm not so sure."

"Lie down," I order. Asher listens, placing his body next to mine on the floor. Our faces still gaze at each other while we remain still on our sides, as though in bed and not in the middle of so much destruction.

"Jade," he whispers, voice wavering. His aura has turned the mocha color of fear. "Don't scare me like that again."

"I have to," I tell him, shaking my head. "The magic is inside of me, Asher. Even now, I want to rip your emotions from your heart, I want to tear them away."

And I do. The magic is pulling at my fingertips, urging me to touch his skin, to remove every ounce of warmth from his body and claim it as my own. But this is Asher. And I could not bear to take his soul from him. Not yet anyway. Eventually though, the magic will win.

Asher takes a deep breath, reaching his hand to my cheek even as I recoil, worried that his touch would be too much to resist. "I told you before, there's another way."

"I'm not going to risk all these people—"

"You won't," he interrupts. I gather my courage, looking into his eyes as they hold me captive. Hope. I'm not sure if it will be my salvation or my demise.

"Asher," I plead, begging him to release me, to let it end.

"No, Jade, listen. I realized it after you left me in my cell. This whole time, the answer has been so obvious, it's been staring us in the face. All we need to do is break the curse."

"Break the curse?" I repeat slowly. I don't understand. "That's what I'm trying to do. I need to kill myself to lift the queen's magic, now my magic."

Asher shakes his head, leaning closer, imploring. "Not that curse, Jade. The original curse. A while ago, I told you magic always starts with a curse. But I was too fixed on my path to realize what that statement meant. It wasn't until I was faced with your death that I understood. The curse brought the magic to my family, so only ending the curse can take it away. Do you understand?"

"I don't have to die?" I ask, shivering, not really clear.

"No," he smiles, shaking his head. "You see, I thought death was the only way, but for the entirely wrong reason. I thought it was because the magic would have no new body to enter, but that's so wrong. If it wanted to, the magic could go anywhere. But the curse, the curse is tied to the bloodline. If you die, the curse would be broken because there would be no heir to inherit it. But there's more than one way to break a curse."

"What's the other way?" I ask. My fingers ache to touch his skin, to feel the happiness burning his cheek, turning his aura a wonderful yellow, as though he were the sun. Or maybe a guardian angel. In paintings, the angels are always depicted in a halo of soft ambient light, too good, too bright for Earth's dull atmosphere.

Asher sits up slowly, leaning over me, placing his hands on either side of my head so I cannot escape. I roll onto my back, gazing up at him. Every nerve in my body is alert. The magic stops pulling for his skin, stops yearning to steal his light. Instead, it stills, waiting with me, wondering if it has finally found its freedom.

"My family's curse was to never find love, to never understand it, to use the magic to take what can never be given to us. Now you're the heir, so it's your curse. But don't you see? We already broke it."

Asher's fingers brush the hair from my face, caressing my skin. He leans down, placing a soft kiss on my forehead, on my nose, on my lips.

"I love you," Asher whispers.

My heart bursts.

His words have shattered it, busted through the ice, the frost, releasing the heat inside. The magic breaks free, ripping through my chest, lifting me partially off the ground as it expels from the cage my body had become. For what feels like the first time in my life, I don't fight. I remain passive, limp, letting everything drain away.

Sparks ripple the air around me, brilliant white light, swirling with the wind. The higher it flies, the fainter it becomes—twinkling magic returning to where it belongs. Free, as I always yearned to be. As I finally am.

My eyes find Asher, watching as the aura around his body mutes, fades away, and then entirely disappears. He still looks like an angel to me.

"Asher," I whisper, voice hoarse as my hand rises to cup his cheek, "I love you."

He smirks, as though he knew my secret all along. I knew his too.

In a flash, our lips are a mere inch apart. I wonder if the burn will be stronger now that I know exactly how he feels, if it is even possible. Already my toes tingle with anticipation, my breath comes uneven, my heart flutters girlishly in my chest.

I close the gap just as a cough sounds at the door.

"Uh, guys?"

Asher and I break apart in a rush. He nearly falls to the floor in surprise and I sit up, narrowly missing his head.

Maddy stands in the doorway, face absently confused, totally blank. But not an emotionless emptiness, more like her mind has cleared, leaving her unsure. My fault, I realize. I completely forgot I used the magic to call her here.

"I, uh..." She shuffles her feet. "I feel like I was coming here for a reason, but, like, I have no idea why all of a sudden."

"Maddy," I breathe, releasing all of the pressure from my chest.

This is not the girl I left on the street a week before. Her voice is full of life, full of the energy that first scared me but I have since come to love, which can only mean one thing.

The curse is broken.

The magic really is gone.

I leave Asher on the ground and run to Maddy, hugging her close. "You have no idea how happy I am to see you."

"Really?" she asks, hugging me back and then leaning away to peer at Asher over my shoulder. "I mean, I was a little worried I interrupted something. You know..." Her cheeks grow pink, and I do know exactly what she's thinking.

But I look over my shoulder at Asher, at his disheveled hair. His eyes are shining brighter than I've ever seen them, as though they hold a magic all their own. We smile at each other, one mind thinking the exact same thing.

"Don't worry." I turn back to Maddy, trying to contain my sudden glee. "Asher and I have all the time in the world."

Twenty-Seven

The city that never sleeps has come back to life.

The curse has only been lifted for a few days, but already the change is palpable. A thrilling charge fills the air, the noise of chatter, of laughter, of cries. Every day a family is reunited, a loved one is found. Every day, the people come more and more back to life.

And the electricity has started working again. Many of the old buildings still don't have power. They are too broken down, too far decayed. The original grid has been completely destroyed by the earthquake and by time. But the rebels brought a few solar panels with them when they marched, so we are connected to the outside world through radios and a few satellite feeds. The calls are nonstop.

Rebels from around the world are reaching out, in awe, in excitement, wondering how we managed to defeat the magic. Asher and I have told the story a hundred times, and we will continue to do so as long as people want to hear it. The first victory in over a decade. The first glimpse of hope.

Dozens of cities around the world are still trapped by other monarchs. We see the magic auras on our maps, pulsing invisible to our radar scans. But that is not what people are paying attention to anymore, at least not right now. Their eyes are focused on New York, on the spot where the magic winked out and a survivor's city was revealed.

I am one of those survivors.

And so is Asher.

Even as my hand grips his, I can hardly believe it. But it's true. Somehow.

"Are you ready?" he asks.

We are standing before the wall, eyes glued to a sight I never thought I would see. This wall was my second home. I've memorized every stone, every bump, every crack. For years, it stood as a symbol of the division between us and them, between rebel and guard, between free and ensnared, between brother and sister.

Now it stands for hope.

Hundreds of pictures cover the gray stone, smiling faces we hope to get back, loved ones we hope to eventually find. Our new missing person's wall. Each day a photo is taken down and each day another replaces it. Though many have been reunited, many more are still lost.

Like the woman I hold in my hand.

My mother.

"Go on," Asher urges, pushing the small of my back just slightly. I step forward, breath tight, hands unsteady. The back of my neck tingles. When I do this, it becomes real—the wish to see her alive, the desire to hold her in my arms, the need to make her understand that I am so very sorry for waiting so long, for forgetting.

I lick my lips. If I'm being honest, those yearnings are real already.

I look down at the photograph in my hands. Her face is slightly different than I remember, more like mine than I realized. Both of our skins are a golden brown, kissed by the sun. Her hair is curlier, but it is clearly where I get my waves. Her eyes are warmer than mine, but colorful, and just as loving as I imagined. My father is in this photo too, though I know he passed before I was born. For the first time, I see myself in him as well. Though his skin is pale, our smile is the same, lips slightly thinner but opening wide. And the curve of my eyes, slightly round, sharp at each end, is just like his. And there are the mixes, the way my hair is a shade in between the jet-black of my father and the light brown of my mother, how my cheekbones are high like his but also defined like hers.

I had forgotten what my parents looked like until yesterday when I found this picture in my hand. The apartment hadn't been touched for years. While I was under the queen's thrall, I never bothered to visit. Partially because

I no longer cared. Partially because I didn't want to face who I had once been and who I had then become.

But Asher and I went back to my home, to a place I thought I would never see again. The building was cracked and broken, definitely unsafe, but the risk was worth it. When we found my apartment, the scene looked frozen in time. My toys were still on the ground. My bed was still unmade. Old plates sat in the sink growing mold. A thick layer of dust covered everything. But underneath I found a few precious treasures. Photo albums, letters, trinkets of jewelry. We took whatever we could carry.

This photograph had been in a frame in her bedroom, but now it will live on the wall, a sign of hope that maybe I will see her again.

With one more deep breath, I attach the picture, adding my mother to the sea of lost faces wishing to be found. Then I step back into Asher's waiting arms. They wrap around me as he places a soft kiss on my neck.

"We'll find her," he promises. The gentle kindness in his voice is just one of the reasons I love him.

"Come on." I take Asher's hand and lead him away. "There's something I want to show you."

"What?"

But I shake my head. It's my turn to surprise him. "You'll see."

A guard tower looms ahead and I sneak him inside. They are barren now that the guard has been disbanded.

Most of my former comrades have joined the rebellion and eagerly await their next assignment, wondering what new city they will help free. But others are content to give up the guns and swords, to help rebuild in different ways. There are more than enough jobs to go around.

Me? I've always been a fighter. At least now, I can fight for something I believe in.

Asher and I climb the steps two at a time and then scamper up to the top ring of the wall, a few stories in the air. I breathe easier up here, away from the noise and commotion, remembering countless hours spent in solitude, relaxed and at peace on my own.

As I turn to make sure Asher is still with me, my feet continue forward, all too used to this path. We're going to my favorite spot on the wall, further toward the west. After we pass through two more guardhouses, I stop, taking in the view.

The crumbling buildings of old New York City look softer in the musty light of sunset. The angles are less harsh. The decay is muted by shadows. The gray is splashed with pinks and oranges, painterly reflections making the city feel more alive, less barren. But that is not why I love this view, it is for the dried up riverbed to my right, the old Hudson River that has since stopped flowing. But the grooves make a deep path, a line to the fading horizon, an arrow to freedom. It's one of the only places on the south side of the wall where you can see for miles, where no tall buildings block your vision. The glimmer of water reflects far in the distance, promising that an endless ocean rests nearby, a gateway to the rest of the world.

I used to stand here and wonder if my feet would ever walk that path, if I would ever be free. But now nothing is stopping me, nothing except the warm fingers clutching my hand, squeezing it affectionately, whispering that I never have to be alone again.

"Is this what you wanted to show me?" Asher asks.

"Sort of." I shrug. "Less of a place and more of an idea."

I tear my eyes from the scene only to realize that Asher has been looking at me the entire time, eyes a soft indigo just like the sky. A smile comes shyly to my lips as blood floods my cheeks. Something in his stare still makes me nervous, excited. I hope the feeling never changes.

"What idea was that?" He smirks, noticing my reaction.

I nudge him lightly on the shoulder. "For the first time, when I look at the world, I see possibilities. Not daydreams. Not fantasies. I see real places I can go. Real people I can save. And it's all because of you."

"I think you had a little something to do with it," he teases, but his eyes are more serious, heartfelt. Tone deeper, Asher adds, "I feel the same way."

I pause, hesitant, but his eyes are warm and welcoming, and I know these are words that need to be said at least once. "I want you to know that I'm sorry—"

"Jade," Asher interrupts, but I press on.

"I'm sorry I killed her," I finish, voice barely even a whisper. "I almost didn't, almost couldn't, because for a moment I saw the woman you always saw, the one who just wanted to be loved. But then I remembered everything she's done, and I just, I just..."

"I know," he murmurs, pulling my head into his chest, running his fingers through my hair. "You only did what you had to do. What I wasn't strong enough to do. And it's okay."

"No, it's not. It's not okay that you're trying to help find my mother when I'm the person who took yours away. But I want you to know that wherever we go next, I'll do whatever I can to make it up to you."

A twitch runs through his body, stilling me, making me pull back.

"Asher?" I ask, but he looks away, suddenly unable to meet my eyes. "What?"

"It's just," he pauses, looking utterly sheepish with eyebrows slightly raised and lips unusually pouted. "There is one thing."

"Anything," I add quickly, confused.

"Well, it's more of a someone."

I'm immediately suspicious. "Who?"

Asher swallows, expression far too apologetic. "A girl. I made a promise when we were children that I wouldn't abandon her, and I just learned she's been trapped by a man the rebels know only as the beast."

"Who is she?" I demand, voice tight. My blood has started to pound, to race. I take a step closer just as Asher steps farther away.

"Her name is Omorose."

"I meant who is she to you?"

"Jade," he pleads, grabbing my shoulders, looking me dead in the eye. "Please remember how much I love you, that I have to be in love with you and only you or the curse never would have lifted."

"Asher," I growl.

He backs away, slowly, inch by inch as though I am a ticking bomb about to explode. "She's my fiancé."

And then he runs.

All the air leaves my body, expelled by pure shock. But then I'm boiling, fuming. My hands ball into fists as my unruly emotions take over.

That jerk.

Then I'm running too.

And we both know it's only a matter of time until I catch him.

Don't miss

Withering Rose

Once Upon a Curse Book Two

The classic fairy tale of *Beauty & The Beast* gets retold—
only this time, beauty is cursed and the beast is the only
one who can save her.

Coming May 2016!

Sign up at the below link to be notified the morning it
goes on-sale!

TinyLetter.com/KaitlynDavisBooks

About The Author

Bestselling author Kaitlyn Davis writes young adult fantasy novels under the name Kaitlyn Davis and contemporary romance novels under the name Kay Marie.

Always blessed with an overactive imagination, Kaitlyn has been writing ever since she picked up her first crayon and is overjoyed to share her work with the world. When she's not daydreaming, typing stories, or getting lost in fictional worlds, Kaitlyn can be found indulging in some puppy videos, watching a little too much television, or spending time with her family.

Connect with the Author Online:

Website: KaitlynDavisBooks.com
Facebook: Facebook.com/KaitlynDavisBooks
Twitter: @DavisKaitlyn
Tumblr: KaitlynDavisBooks.tumblr.com
Wattpad: Wattpad.com/KaitlynDavisBooks
Goodreads: Goodreads.com/Kaitlyn_Davis

CPSIA information can be obtained
at www.ICGtesting.com
Printed in the USA
LVOW08s0039091116
512211LV00007B/167/P